I0708321

TRANQUILITY MOON

WHERE VIOLENCE HAS NO VOICE

TOM SKORE

TRANQUILITY MOON

WHERE VIOLENCE HAS NO VOICE

CITIOFBOOKS, INC.
3736 Eubank NE Suite A1
Albuquerque, NM 87111-3579
www.citiofbooks.com
Hotline: 1 (877) 389-2759
Fax: 1 (505) 930-7244

Ordering Information:

Quantity sales. Special discounts are available on quantity purchases by corporations, associations, and others. For details, contact the publisher at the address above.

Printed in the United States of America.

ISBN-13:   Softcover   979-8-89391-950-9
                eBook   979-8-89391-952-3
                Hardback   979-8-89391-951-6

Library of Congress Control Number: 2025920644

"When Thoughts and Prayers Are Not Enough"

TRANQUILITY MOON

The young girl's father had been in space for well over two months already, but what made it bearable were the video conferences to the International Space Station once a week and the one cell phone call allowed midweek. She was grateful for these opportunities, but it still didn't feel like enough, even though she knew this mission was supposed to be simulating a trip to Mars, during which contact with families would be quite limited. For the girl's father, Paul Connors, the mission was as much a psychological test as a test of physical stamina. The plan was for her dad to break the previous endurance record for the most time spent in space, at least eighteen months, with a couple more tacked on to the end to test the psychological effects of something going wrong as it might on a long voyage. That decision would depend on ground control's assessment of her dad's overall state of mind at that time.

On those days when she wasn't scheduled to call, the girl took delight in peering through the telescope her dad had bought for her, which was powerful enough to give a clear image of the space station, the moon, Venus, Mars, and even the gas giants Saturn and Jupiter.

This particular day had been a distressing one for the girl. Like all the kids in her fifth-grade class, she enjoyed the occasional day off from school. But the reason she was back home on this particular day was because there had been an active shooter incident with the loss of several lives at the high school her brother attended, which was adjacent to the charter school where she was a student. Fortunately her brother, who called her shortly after the incident occurred, was all right. But she still found the experience disconcerting and frightening, having happened so close to home and family. It was hard not to think about the distinct possibility that it could have been her, her brother, or one of her classmates. And while she didn't have any friends at the high school yet, and suspected she did not know any of the dead or injured, she still prayed for everyone involved.

Though not a day on which she would normally expect to hear from her father, she was excited to see her dad's picture pop up when her cell phone rang. Under the circumstances Capcom granted the astronaut permission to call, and his daughter was grateful to hear her father's calm and reassuring voice. The girl surprised herself when she burst into tears, overwhelmed by a torrent of emotion she didn't even know was in her.

"Sorry, Dad," the girl said, trying to steady her voice. "I don't mean to worry you."

"You have nothing to apologize for, sweetheart. I heard the news reports, even up here. It sounded like a terrible ordeal." Her father was peering down at Earth as he floated in space while speaking to his daughter.

"It was, Dad. They don't even know how many were shot yet. I'm still shaking a little."

"But you're all right?"

"Yes. I think. So is Nick. He called me right after it happened."

"I know. Your brother called me too. He said he was fine, but he wasn't. McKenzie, the girl he used to be so fond of, was seriously wounded, and he was understandably very angry."

"Nick didn't tell me about McKenzie. I really liked her."

"So did I," Paul said plaintively. "Is your mom with you?"

"No, Dad, not yet. She was in surgery but relayed a message that she would be home just as soon as she could get here."

"You hang in there, Rianne. If you want to, you call your grandmother or your aunt Becca and talk to them until your mom or your brother gets home. Or call me back if you need to."

"I will, Dad."

"I'm sorry I can't be with you, Sweetheart."

"I know, Dad. I understand. I'm proud of what you're doing. All my friends think it's so cool that my dad's an astronaut."

"Cool as it is, I'd rather be with you right now."

"I know, Dad."

"We'll be passing over you in about ten minutes. Maybe you can catch a glimpse with your telescope."

"I'll do that, Dad."

"You take care. And try to get some sleep."

"I love you, Dad." The girl started to well up again.

"I love you too, Sweetheart."

The girl ended the call, sad that it was over. Her dad was a steady, calm influence, something that came with the training.

Something that the job demanded. She hoped to follow in her dad's footsteps one day.

Rianne looked across her room at the telescope, mounted on the tripod near the window. It was near twilight by now and the evening stars were beginning to shine. A nearly full moon was also making its presence felt and the girl thought to look through the telescope for a while to get her mind off the shock of the day. She liked gazing upward. Looking at the space station always helped her feel a little bit closer to her dad. Rianne spent a lot of time by herself. That's what having a surgeon for a mom, an astronaut for a dad, and an older brother in high school was all about. But in all ways she felt she had the world's best family and it was her intention never to disappoint them or break their faith in her good judgment.

Looking through the telescope eyepiece, it didn't take her long to find the space station. Even with a fairly powerful telescope, it was still relatively small, but she always kept a mental picture in the back of her mind as to where it was, or where it would be at any given moment in time. Keeping track was a way of keeping close. While grateful that the sky was clear, on this particular night, the view was still a little more tricky than usual due to the station's proximity to the nearly full moon, with bright sunlight reflecting off its rocky surface. Since Rianne could not make out much detail on the space station under the circumstances, she decided to turn her attention to the moon itself.

Rianne always found the moon to be infinitely fascinating. She found Mars to be infinitely fascinating too, as well as the moons of Saturn and Jupiter and their immense potential for life. However, they had never known a human's footsteps. Her heroes were Neil Armstrong and Walt Disney, in that order. The kid in her loved and admired Disney's creative vision, particularly princesses, and strong female heroes. But the young woman in her thought being the first person to set foot on another world was beyond anything she could imagine feeling. Truly it was something worth risking your life for and to be remembered for.

Rianne also admired the technological advances space ventures had historically brought about. These were not *Star Wars* and *Star Trek* fantasies but hard-core realities that made her life better every day. And in the process the universe was constantly revealing more of its secrets. And her father was a big part of it, and she wanted to be a part of it too.

Rianne trained her telescope where the sunlight met the darkness on the moon's surface. The contrast between the two brought amazing clarity as the sunlight bounced off the various rock formations, creating shadows that made for an almost 3-D effect. It was hard to believe that the light she was seeing was coming from the sun and not from some subsurface light source. It was hard to think, as scientists now suspected, that this object had once been part of the earth itself, torn away by some cataclysmic impact. Now it was like the earth's dance partner, only this dance partner had stopped spinning, slowed by the earth's gravitational field. The earth's rotation was slowing too, seemingly brokenhearted because its partner was pulling away, showing only one side of its face forever more.

Rianne knew it was silly to attribute such thoughts to two huge chunks of floating space rock, but then again she had gained newfound appreciation for the earth through her father's work—for its beauty—and an understanding of the peril it is facing. Climate change was still a major challenge, and global political instability was always a worry. Not that she knew the ins-and-outs, but she could sense her parents' concerns and it rubbed off on her. Rianne's teachers talked about these things in school but she always sensed they were cautious in what they expressed, worried that some students came from families with differing political views. Many felt that grade school was about learning basic skills: reading, writing, and math. It was not an appropriate forum for philosophical debates about politics and the like. She was thankful that she was able to get some of that at home. It made her feel a couple of steps ahead of her classmates, especially the boys who spoke of little beyond sports, games, movies, and social media.

Rianne kept scanning the moon's surface as all these thoughts continued whizzing through her head. She had looked over everything of interest—twice—and was ready to go downstairs for a bite to eat when something caught her eye. It wasn't much. It wasn't even on the surface. But it was big enough and intense enough to see, and then it wasn't there. But in Rianne's mind there was no disputing it had been there, and it shouldn't have been.

For a moment she felt incredible excitement. Then reality dawned and she felt enormous fear. There was also a moment when she doubted what she saw. When that passed, she realized how hard it would be to get anyone to believe her.

Rianne couldn't imagine what she had seen. It had to be fairly large for her to be able to pick it out so near to the bright edge of the moon's surface. It was moving so slowly it was hard for her to believe it was orbiting the moon. In fact, it didn't seem to be going around at all. Rather, it appeared to stop momentarily and then disappear behind the moon, but it was surely no meteor or space rock. Not moving that slowly. Not moving in a controlled manner like that. She knew these things from discussions she had many times with her father.

Determined to find answers, Rianne decided to forego dinner and keep looking through the telescope. In reality she was assuming it was nothing more than her eyes playing tricks on her, but in any case she decided to wait and see if this ghost would reappear on the opposite side of the moon and provide her with a few answers. As a precaution, and for proof's sake, she decided to hook her pink Galaxy phone (it had to be a Galaxy!) to the telescope so she could record the anomaly should it reappear. This way if it were something of interest, she would have documentation to share with her dad, who she knew would be the only person to take her seriously at all.

It had been some time since Rianne had started her vigil, but she had seen nothing more. She was startled when she heard the garage door opening. She thought it might be her brother, but it wasn't long before she heard the sound of her mother's voice calling her name.

"Rianne?"

"In my room, Mom."

Rianne kept the scope trained on the opposite side of the moon at the same approximate latitude at which she first spotted the object under the assumption that if what she saw *was* an orbiting body, it would appear within a reasonable period of time, but she was fast losing hope. She heard her mother's footsteps approach and then looked up as her bedroom door swung open, Rianne's arm bumping the telescope slightly as she did so.

"Shoot!"

"Please don't say that," her mom said as she entered Rianne's room.

"Why?"

"Not after what happened at the school today." Rianne's mom, Dr. Lisa Franklin-Connors, had responded rather more sharply than she intended. The cardiothoracic surgeon was usually mild mannered, but the day's events had left an indelible impression that she knew she would never forget.

"I didn't mean anything by it, Mom. I just bumped my telescope."

"I'm sorry, sweetheart. I'm just tired. Are you all right?" Lisa stood in front of Rianne, her hands clasping her daughter's arms, as though inspecting her for damage.

"I'm fine, Mom. It was at the high school that the shootings happened. Not my school."

"I know, but it was right next door. I was in surgery, operating on one of the victims."

"I know. The hospital gave me the message. But I didn't know you were treating someone who got shot."

"Yes. She's still in critical condition."

"Was it McKenzie?"

"Yes. How did you know?"

"Dad told me."

"When did you talk to him?"

"Just a little while ago. He said Nick called him and was really upset."

"He was. Nick was still hanging out at the hospital when I left. He wanted to be there if she regained consciousness."

"But they broke up, didn't they?"

"Yes, they did, sweetheart, but that doesn't necessarily mean you stop caring."

"I know," Rianne responded. "I just thought she probably had a new boyfriend by now."

"I didn't see anyone else there but Nick and McKenzie's immediate family. But I think it's going to be quite a while before she's able to talk to anyone."

"That bad, huh?"

"It's pretty bad," Lisa said, sounding very disheartened. "How about you? Are you sure you're okay?"

"Maybe a little shaky," the young girl admitted. "We could hear the shots. It was kind of scary."

"I'm sure, sweetheart. More than 'kind of scary.' I'm sure it was horrible. I'm sorry I wasn't able to be here with you."

"It's okay, Mom. You were helping people. And Dad's call helped."

"Well that's good. I know it certainly makes me feel better when I talk to your father."

"I cried at first. I was a little surprised and embarrassed, but Dad told me to hang in there. He said he loved me and wished he could be with me and that I should call Grandma or Aunt Becca if I needed before you or Nick came home. Or to call him back. You know Dad. He's always cool."

"Yes, he is." Lisa smiled and then asked, "Did you eat yet?"

"No."

"Why not? I left food."

"I know. But I wasn't really hungry before."

"Understandable. How about now?"

"Maybe a little."

"Why don't you come downstairs with me, and I'll fix us something."

"I'd like to stay up here a while longer, if that's okay?"

"Why?" her mom asked, surprised that Rianne wanted to be by herself with all that had happened.

"I'm not sure." Rianne paused a moment, looked at the telescope, and then added, "I thought I saw something," a bit of apprehension seeping into her voice.

"What were you looking at? The space station?" Lisa's voice was carrying a hint of alarm.

"No. The moon. I was looking at the station, but the moon was so bright I started looking at the moon instead, and then I saw something."

"What?"

"I don't know," Rianne said apprehensively. "But it didn't seem natural."

"What do you mean?" her mom persisted.

"It wasn't natural. Like a meteor, or . . . I don't know. I could see it with my eye. It glowed for a moment and then kind of slowly disappeared around back, and I haven't seen it again."

"Maybe it was just a reflection or something."

"Probably. Maybe," her daughter pondered. "Still, I'd like to look for it for a while longer, just in case."

"That's fine. I'll get supper on the table for us and then call you, okay?"

"Okay."

"Looks like I have two space explorers on my hands." Rianne smiled at the thought, and then her mom added, "Rianne. I am so grateful you and your brother are both safe. What happened today was just terrible. It should never happen."

Rianne's mom shut the door, and after a moment, Rianne turned her attention back to the telescope. She was going to swivel it back to where she had positioned it originally before bumping it, but as she looked through the eyepiece, to her astonishment, she saw the anomaly again, or something very much like it. It was a stroke of luck, and this time she would record it before whatever it was disappeared. She quickly pressed the video button on her Galaxy.

The week that followed was a difficult one. Eight students had been killed, and another nine injured, in the horrific shooting the previous week. The same calls to do something to stop the violence went out by the grieved students and parents. The same excuses for nonaction were offered up by politicians and gun-rights advocates. It all made little sense to Rianne, who wasn't even sure her father had a gun. She never saw one, nor had it come up in conversation. But her father had been in the Marine Corps before entering the astronaut program for the private space consortium, and she assumed he had been trained in weaponry. But while her father was very open about almost all subjects, discussions concerning his involvement in the Middle East wars were ended quickly, usually with a disapproving glance from her mother, indicating that it was time for Rianne and Nick to move the conversation in a new direction.

School was canceled for the entire week following the school shootings so students could recover and regroup and those who wanted could attend their fallen classmates' funerals. On the following Saturday, Rianne, Nick, and Lisa attended the funeral for the brother of McKenzie Phillips, the young girl on whom Lisa had performed surgery. McKenzie was still in intensive care, and while her condition had stabilized somewhat, there were still several major obstacles to overcome. However, despite the hospital's best efforts, McKenzie's younger brother had lost his battle. Dr. Lisa Franklin-Connors was no stranger to death, but these deaths were so senseless, with victims so young, she found them extremely difficult to accept.

As they sat at the funeral, Lisa kept thinking about the devastating effect the news of McKenzie's brother's death, something the young girl was bound to question her parents about in the not-too-distant future, might have on McKenzie's own recovery. Lisa didn't want to think about the possibility of McKenzie's parents losing both of their children. As their daughter's surgeon, Lisa could "encourage" the parents to withhold that information for as long as possible, but in the end it was not her call to make.

On their way back to the car after the funeral, Lisa remarked on what a beautiful service it was, but Nick flared. As far as he was concerned McKenzie's brother did not deserve to die, and in defiance decided to walk back to the hospital rather than accept his mother's offer to give him a ride. Since the shootings the tall, lanky, sixteen-year-old had been coming home late at night, and leaving first thing in the morning, so worried about his former girlfriend that he couldn't bear to be anywhere but the hospital. Lisa felt bad because she had been afforded so little opportunity to speak with her son about what had transpired or how he was feeling. But the physician in her figured it was best to leave him alone other than offering him support should he need it. McKenzie's circumstance seemed to be keeping his mind occupied, and that was probably a good thing in terms of his own head. When he was ready, Nick would come around. Lisa was sure of it.

For a long time on the drive home, Rianne sat in silence. Her mom didn't press her, figuring Rianne just needed some personal space to process events. It seemed like every generation Lisa knew of had its own scourge to come to grips with. Hitler and WWII, Korea, Vietnam, the Cold War, terrorism—the list seemed endless. She felt like she had grown up in an era of relative calm and prosperity when she turned eighteen in 1999. Then the shootings at Columbine High School happened, and the world seemed to change forever. At first she thought the Columbine killings were a one-time occurrence, but it didn't take long before Lisa realized something seemed to be going wrong in society at large. People were dying in high schools, colleges, movie theaters; at churches and on the streets—shot, stabbed, run over, or blown up. Clearly it seemed like no place or no one was safe. And of course there was the ultimate expression of hatred and depravity—9/11. She looked over at Rianne and could only pray for her daughter's safety and hope her life would be long and full. Suddenly Rianne spoke up.

"Why do people kill, Mom?"

"You mean why do they kill other people?"

"Yes," the girl responded innocently.

"Sometimes they have to, Ri. Because of war."

"But how about when there aren't any wars?"

"I don't know, Ri," Lisa answered with a mother's understanding and patience. "Because they're ill."

"Then why don't they see a doctor?"

"Some may. But most probably don't know they are ill."

"But they want to kill somebody. How could they not know they're ill?"

"Because they see the world from inside their head, and they're not seeing clearly. They might be delusional, or schizophrenic. Maybe they feel powerful, and they're afraid a doctor would make them feel not-so powerful. Besides, most people don't like to think they need a doctor in that way."

"I don't understand."

"They believe the way they think is perfectly fine; that they don't need anybody's help. Especially a doctor's. In fact, for some people killing may make them feel really *good*, at least momentarily."

"How can that be?" the young girl said, clearly perplexed.

"It's complicated. Why do you like chocolate? Or winning a video game."

"Well, I like chocolate because it tastes good. And I like winning video games because"—she paused a moment—"it sucks to lose!"

Her mom smiled and added, "Elegantly put," and then pursued her point. "Eating chocolate or winning a game also releases chemicals in your brain that make you feel better. One is called dopamine. Whenever you do something you like, your brain releases dopamine, and it makes you feel good. It's called a reward. It's okay when it's for something good, like eating chocolate or winning a soccer game. But when it's for something bad . . ."

"Like killing."

"Could be. But it can also reward people for taking drugs or gambling or stealing or"—she paused—"killing."

"That's creepy. So people can get off on killing other people?"

"Apparently."

"Why don't they put them in jail?"

"Because we don't always know who they are beforehand. It's assumed that people who kill for no apparent reason are mentally ill, and of course they are, but they may not have been in the years prior to killing. Mental illness can be a moving target."

"How do you mean?"

"A person can be fine for years; then for some reason, perhaps they go to war, or they lose a spouse or a job, and they enter a depressive state. They haven't done anything wrong in their whole life, but they have a gun; perhaps they're a hunter, or they keep one for protection, or a youngster might steal one from their parents, and suddenly they shoot someone, because for some reason they're angry."

"With who?"

"With whom, Ri. Who knows? The world maybe. But they're angry. They feel powerless, and the shooting makes that individual feel somehow in control, which is totally false. But that's what they feel. I'm not saying that is how everyone feels, but I think it might be an example of how it is for some people."

"So you're saying that anybody could be a killer at any time."

"I think most people are pretty stable most of the time. But there are biological and psychological reasons people sometimes get derailed. I think the most important thing is to treat everyone you meet with kindness and appreciate the ones you love." Lisa was trying her best to sound hopeful.

"I suppose. And watch your back," her daughter added.

"Yes. And watch your back."

"Did dad ever have to kill anyone? Is that why you tell me not to ask him questions about the war?"

"I think that if and when the time is ever right, that is something you should talk to him about."

"How will I know?"

"Because your dad will bring it up. His experience is personal and was difficult, and he loves you, and when he feels you are old enough to understand, he may tell you."

"So he thinks that I am just a kid?"

"He *respects* the fact that you are just a kid. You should appreciate that, because being a kid won't last forever. So enjoy it while you've got it."

Rianne seemed puzzled but satisfied. Besides, her ten-year-old mind had already moved on ahead to the videoconference they would make to her father as soon as they arrived back at the house.

Paul was glad to get the call from his family. Lisa hadn't had a chance to talk to the astronaut since the school shootings because she had been on call at the hospital so much. On top of that, Paul had been busy with several scientific experiments that were fairly time critical. To the astronaut it seemed ironic that he felt safer in outer space than his son probably felt at school.

"It's so good to see your face, Paul," Lisa said near tears as his image came up on the computer screen.

"Yours too. Like the sunrise."

"You flatterer!"

"Where are the kids?"

"Rianne will be here in a minute or two. I think she was aware we hadn't spoken in several days and wanted to give us a little private time. Or 'squishy time' as she calls it."

"Funny," Paul laughed.

"Yes. Nick, on the other hand, won't be joining us today."

"Why?" Paul asked, clearly disappointed.

"He's with McKenzie."

"How's he coping?" Paul inquired with genuine concern.

"I'm not sure. We haven't had a chance to talk much, even though he's been at the hospital practically nonstop. He drops by my office occasionally, but between my schedule and his anger, connecting with him in any meaningful way has been difficult."

"Anger over the shooting, you mean?"

"Oh, yes," Lisa said emphatically. "I confess I am a little concerned. I've never seen him so withdrawn."

"Could be signs of PTSD," Paul suggested.

"It's a little soon to tell, but I'll be watching," Lisa assured him.

"And Rianne? How's she doing?"

"I think she's doing better than I am, although she is asking some fairly probing questions."

"Like what?"

"Like what you would expect at a time like this. Life and death things."

"Which I am sure you handled just fine."

"I hope so. It's so hard to help your child make sense of senselessness when you can't even do it for yourself."

"I know. I have no doubt that of the two of us, you have the hardest job. And you make the most money," Paul said, trying to lighten the conversation.

"That may be," she said, grinning, "but you're the most famous."

Lisa heard Rianne in the hallway, coming from her bedroom. When she entered, she had her Galaxy smartphone in hand. Lisa had totally forgotten the events of several nights ago.

Rianne had shown Lisa her video, but Lisa didn't take it all that seriously, in part because she was tired and in part because the images were so fuzzy as to be nearly indistinct. However, Lisa also knew that they were important to Rianne and so was happy to give up some time to her so she could show her father. Lisa didn't figure they would arouse much interest, but she knew Paul would be supportive of Rianne's efforts, and that was something that Rianne needed right now.

"Hi, Dad," Rianne said as she sat down next to Lisa.

"Hey, Ri. How's it going?"

"It's okay. I start going back to school in a couple of days, but I wish I wasn't. It's all kind of creepy. Mom and I just went to McKenzie's brother's funeral."

"I'm sorry about that, Rianne. I wish I could say I understand how you feel, but I don't. How could I? You were the ones who lived through it, and it's something you and your brother will carry with you all your lives. But I can tell you that your mother and I are proud of how you've both handled yourselves."

"Thanks, Dad."

There was a long pause, and then Lisa stepped into the conversation and changed the direction.

"I think Rianne has something to show you, Paul."

"What is it, Ri?"

Rianne held her Galaxy cell phone up to the computer's camera. "It's a picture. A video. It's not real good, but I took it the other night when I was looking through the telescope. It's of something I saw near the moon. I saw it twice, and it seemed unnatural. I thought you might be interested."

"Well, of course I am." Paul was squinting as he tried to make out the image on the smaller screen. "The image is a little hard to discern on my screen, Ri. Could you download it to me so I can take a closer look?"

"Sure, Dad," Rianne said, excited that her dad was taking some interest. "I'll do that right away." She turned and headed out of the room.

"Rianne," her father called out, hoping to have a little more time with his daughter. "We could talk a little longer, you know. There's plenty of time for that."

"I know, but I want you to have this right away, Dad."

"Okay. I love you, sweetheart."

"Love you too, Dad," the girl said as she disappeared from sight.

"She's so excited," Lisa said. "You were so nice to her."

"I'm sure it's nothing, but I know my interest is important. I just didn't think it would end the conversation so abruptly."

"Be happy. You're a good dad."

"And you're a good mom—and surgeon."

"I love you, Paul."

"I love you too, Lisa. This is going to be a long stint up here."

"It will be a long stint down here too. But it's nice to know you'll be watching over us every ninety minutes."

"That I will. Always. I'll talk to you in a few days, love."

"All my explorers seem to be rushing out on me."

"Not by choice. Not this one in any case."

"You be safe, Paul. "

"Same to you." Then after a long look at Lisa's face, Paul ended the call with, "Bye."

The screen went blank, and Lisa could feel tears welling up in her eyes, but fought to suppress them as best she could. They had not even made it to the one-eighth mark in terms of the time Paul was to spend in space, and it was just too soon to start giving in to her feelings.

Rianne had sent Paul the video stream, but in reality viewing it was not at the top of his list of priorities. By now he'd had it for a couple of days, and so when Rianne and Lisa next called midweek via cell phone, he could tell Rianne was severely disappointed. Paul decided then and there that he needed to adjust his priorities. Even in space family needed to come first—whenever possible.

It wasn't until Paul saw the image on a larger screen that he understood why Rianne was so adamant about sending it. While the image was not the best, it was clear enough to conclude that whatever it was should not have been there. It was also clear enough to discern that it was not a naturally occurring object.

At first it appeared to be just a glint of light. That could of course be a mere reflection, except it moved, then stood still, and then moved again, finally disappearing around the far side of the moon. There was also a kind of rippled, slightly wavy distortion surrounding the object, only briefly discernable near the edge of the moon. Rianne had also stated that she had seen whatever it was twice, and though she was unable to record it the first time, there was no reason to doubt his daughter's veracity. Like his daughter, Paul wasn't sure what to make of it, and like his daughter, he knew he couldn't let this go.

The space station had a formidable telescope of its own, and Paul's first thought was to use it. The Celestron, Hyper-Star equipped, computerized Pathfinder telescope, part of the station's ISERV system, was used primarily for monitoring events on Earth, like hurricanes and rain-forest destruction. It wasn't exactly portable but could potentially be moved about the station to another window if there were good cause. It would present problems, however, because either the station was positioned to take pictures of Earth, its rotation set so that it always faced the planet, or it could be positioned to take pictures of space but couldn't do both at the same time. In its current configuration, the station was simply moving too fast to get clear images of astronomical objects. But Galaxy Enterprises' mission-control science team might have a solution for that. Before speaking with them, however, Paul decided to first call Rianne, not only to congratulate her but to ask her about what she had seen the first time or if she had seen anything else since recording the video. Paul was realizing that his daughter had become a de facto part of their team and was secretly beaming with pride.

"No, Dad. I only saw it those two times," the young girl responded to his question. "The first time it looked about the same as the second. I thought it might come out on the opposite side of the moon, but I waited forever, and it never did. I only saw it in that one spot."

"What do you think? Was this the same object you saw the first time, or might it have been another one?"

"Gee, Dad, I never thought of that. They looked the same. But I don't know."

"If they were different objects, it might be even more crucial to find out what's going on."

"What do you think it is?" Rianne asked her dad with a mixture of fascination and fear.

"To tell you the truth, Ri, I have no idea. But clearly something is going on up there, and something is behind it. I plan on passing this along to NASA and our Galaxy mission commanders. Could be they already know it's there. I'm hoping to take a look myself through our onboard ISERV system. I can probably get a clearer image if there's anything to see. But I'll need to clear it with mission control first."

"Cool, Dad."

"I'll let you know soon as I hear anything. That is, if it isn't classified."

"You think it could be?"

"It could be, but I don't want to jump the gun here. I'm sure the experts will come up with a logical explanation, but it does look a little unusual. You did real good, sweetheart."

"Thanks, Dad."

"And, Rianne, I need you to promise me that you won't tell anyone. If it proves to be nothing at all, there's no point in arousing people's fear. And if it *is* something . . ."

"There's still no point in arousing people's fear. I understand, Dad."

"That's my girl. I'll get back to you soon." With that, Rianne's computer screen went blank.

The group that Paul flew for, Galaxy Enterprises, was a consortium of private firms, each involved with some aspect of space exploration. Sparked by the initial successes of companies like Elon Musk's Space X, the consortium was now a web of intertwined enterprises, each with its own specialty but all committed to the human exploration of space. Profits for these tech firms came primarily in the form of patents generated by their R&D departments and the products manufactured by their subsidiary companies for public consumption. As the public began enjoying the rewards of all the new scientific advancements brought on by this renewed activity, interest in space exploration regained some of the enthusiasm that had been lost after the Apollo missions of the 1960s and '70s and the cancellation of the Space Shuttle program. But for all of that, there were still major funding hurdles for space exploration to overcome. Pressing problems like climate change, social inequality, and nuclear proliferation dominated many people's agendas, particularly the politicians'. These issues were all deemed more important than putting humans on other worlds. But slowly, the private space industry was beginning to show signs of profitability, and NASA was becoming more accepting of working across the boards with private firms to achieve mutual ends.

Paul had relayed Rianne's video to his mission controllers. As Paul had done, they had put it on the back burner, and it was several days before they got back to him. But when they did, there was no mistaking the level of alarm they were feeling.

"You say your daughter took this video?"

"That's right."

"What kind of telescope?"

"Eighty mm, off-the-shelf refractor. I bought it for her before I came up here so she could see the ISS from the ground. She's becoming quite the little scientist."

The Galaxy mission commander was Ken Ishida, a no-nonsense but likable former Marine in his late forties with a calm demeanor and a wealth of ideas. Later trained at Stanford, MIT, and Princeton, he had multiple areas of expertise in astrophysics, cosmology, quantum mechanics, and rocketry. As such it was a surprise to Paul that there was a distinct sense of urgency in Ken's voice. "We want to do some follow-up," Ken said abruptly.

"Okay," Paul said, not certain as to where this was going.

"Ideally it would be great to get the Hubble on this," Ken continued, "but I think we need to take some incremental steps first."

"Have you looked with any larger ground-based telescopes?" Paul asked.

"I'm not sure that would tell us much, in that the distortions could be caused by the earth's atmosphere. I'm thinking it would be much better for you to use your onboard system and see what you come up with before we ask that the Hubble or the JWST to be repositioned. We know so little at this moment I think it's better to keep this in-house."

"Understood. But you know we'd have to use the onboard thrusters to totally reorient the station. NASA is going to have to be told."

"I know," Ken said reluctantly. "But I think we need to find out what's going on, ASAP."

"You sound worried."

"I am. Whatever it is that I saw was more than likely human-made, at least I hope so. If it is we need to find out who is doing it and what they are doing. This is technology we haven't seen in any space program, except our own, and I don't even think *we* could do what I saw. We need to find out if the Chinese or the Russians are way out in front of us."

"Do we have any reason to suspect they are?" Paul questioned.

"Not that I know of. And that's the point."

"And if it isn't them?" Paul said with some trepidation.

"I wouldn't even speculate at this point. I don't think there are any other plausible candidates. But first we want to set you up so you can take a look from the space station. At least then we'll know if the distortions are being caused by the earth's atmosphere or are due to the anomaly itself. I'll also get our team working on it down here and see if anyone knows of anything that's been developed that could account for an object to be maneuvered in that way. That's what's got my heart pounding."

"We'll get right on it up here," Paul assured him.

Ken's image disappeared from the screen, and all Paul could think of in that moment was what would he tell his daughter.

By the next day, the ground technicians had determined the best window to set up the Celestron, which would require the least amount of maneuvering of the space station itself to acquire a clear image of the moon. Fortunately it would be set up in the US portion of the space station, but Paul was sure the Russians would ask an abundance of questions since the whole station would require reorientation. He got along well with his cosmonaut friends, but he was unsure if they had been alerted to what was going on or perhaps knew themselves *exactly* what was going on.

While the solution that the Galaxy mission-control team provided for the placement of the telescope was a fairly manageable one, in space nothing was really, truly easy. Moving a fairly large object within tight confines, in zero gravity, presented multiple risks. And once it was set up, it was probably going to take time to pinpoint the anomaly, if it was there to see at all. No doubt, with the station moving so fast, getting a steady, clear image was going to be difficult. It was also undecided as to how long they should pursue such a search. Rianne, who found the anomaly by accident, had only seen it twice, and deep down in his heart, Paul still had numerous lingering doubts that there was really anything there.

While it would have been nice to use the ISERV system's digital capabilities and put it on automatic, the fact that the space station was in constant motion, and the object they were supposedly looking for so small in comparison, made it necessary for the astronauts to do more manual manipulation of the telescope. NASA in particular, by now having been brought up to speed on the situation, was looking for answers. But there were so many chores and other scientific projects vying for attention that the time the crew could actually spend nursing the telescope was limited. The fact that the moon was in an optimum position for viewing only once every ninety minutes or so did not make things any easier, as it interrupted the other tasks the astronauts were required to perform.

They had been spending what time they could over the course of several days when Martina Gimanni, an Italian astronaut, spotted another anomaly near the moon, even more perplexing than the one Rianne had seen. With Paul tucked away in another part of the station, working on a scientific experiment, Martina called to him over the intercom.

By the time Paul got to her, the anomaly had disappeared around the backside of the moon, but Martina was able to record the image for him to see. In this case, while there was still an element of light associated with it, rather than the typical fiery flash they would expect to see from a rocket engine, what they saw in this case was a sustained faint bluish glow that seemed to be descending toward the moon, but from the far side, and from quite a distance away. Nor was it an orbital trajectory, but it was a controlled stop-and-start descent, with pronounced directional adjustments. And the same distortions that had been evident in Rianne's video were discernable as the anomaly swept past the field of stars in the background. Based on what they were seeing, there was little doubt that this was either a human-made object or something made by an intelligence from somewhere else. In either case there was ample cause for alarm.

"What do you think?" Paul asked Martina, perhaps hoping she had a plausible explanation.

"I think I now know how Galileo felt when he first saw the moons of Jupiter," she said. "He knew there was going to be trouble and that things would never be the same."

"Roger that," Paul replied. Then after a moment, "Let's get these images to Ken."

Ken Ishida's team was composed of a wonderfully odd assortment of technical whizzes, some barely more than kids, at least from Ken's point of view. There was no denying their brilliance, on the one hand, and no denying that they were in these jobs for the fun as well as the challenge. While they all took their jobs seriously, their senses of humor were always on display, and in this situation it was no different.

Their first responses were filled with "cool" and references to ETs. Someone was humming the theme to Rod Serling's *Twilight Zone*, but as they got down to business, a different tone permeated the room. As they watched the video over and over, there was a realization on their part that something unusual was happening on the moon and that it looked like it wasn't coming from Earth.

"Whatever it is definitely appears to be approaching from outside the orbit of the moon," said John Wilner, one of the senior scientists.

"I agree," said Teddy Brower, a geeky, gangly young man with curly hair and thick black-rimmed glasses. "It also appears to be cloaked, like a stealth aircraft designed to avoid radar detection."

"Not cloaked," said Wilner, interrupting Teddy. "It appears to be some kind of metamaterial rendering it invisible."

"You're right," agreed Teddy without taking offense. "And I would venture a guess that if these images had not been taken from the ISS, we might not have seen them at all."

"How so?" asked Ken.

"Because it would have been totally masked from Earth by the moon," Teddy responded.

"Wouldn't they have done that from the start?" a young female scientist, Julian Ames, chimed in.

"What do you mean?" Ken probed.

"When Paul's daughter first recorded the images she took," Julian said, "she was on Earth. Wouldn't' they have masked their presence then?"

"Maybe they're not masking their presence at all. Maybe they could care less if we see them or not," Teddy persisted.

"Or maybe they were doing something on the face of the moon, on the near side, and, just by happenstance, happened to get caught," Wilner speculated.

"Clearly a lot of conjecture going on here with very little to back it up," Ken said, frustrated by the lack of any clear answers or guidance. "I need some suggestions as to where we go from here."

"I think we should consider a full range of options: infrared, gamma ray, x-ray, ultraviolet. See if there is a heat source, and what kind," said Wilner.

"What about the James Webb Space Telescope?" Ames asked.

"I think under the circumstances it's appropriate to ask about the JWST," said Ken. "I'll be sending what we have over to

NASA as soon as we're finished here. In the meantime we'll keep monitoring as best we can. Anything else?" Ken inquired.

"You know, it's kind of funny," Ames said after a moment, her voice a little shaky. "All your life you're watching movies about aliens. Good aliens. Nasty, bad aliens. But somehow in the back of your mind, you never really think it will ever happen. At least not in your lifetime. But here we are, it's happening, or at least it might be, and to tell you the truth, I'm a little bit scared."

The others looked around the silent room, obviously feeling quite similar.

"Amen to that," said Ken. "Let's get to work."

Several days later Paul was waiting to call home, in a quandary about what to say concerning the latest developments. In actuality he wasn't even sure what they all added up to. The consortium had optical telescopes focused on the moon but had seen nothing, while NASA's airborne infrared telescopes indicated that there was definitely a strong heat source on the backside surface of the moon, its electromagnetic output strong enough to be seen as a halo around the moon's edges. Clearly, something was generating massive amounts of energy on the far side of the moon, but neither NASA's LRO nor a host of other orbiting satellites from the United States, and multiple foreign countries, were able to identify the actual source. The only conclusion one could draw was that it was being generated by something extremely powerful, and though the moon had a molten core, as far as anyone knew, there was not enough tectonic activity to account for it. Meteor impact was ruled out, even though impacts on the far side of the moon are far more frequent than the near side, because the energy output was far too steady.

Paul still hadn't determined what to tell his family when their faces lit up his computer screen, beating him to the videoconference.

"How are you all doing?" he said, having some difficulty switching mental gears.

"We're good, Paul," Lisa answered.

"Great, Dad," Rianne chimed in.

"Hey, Dad," Nick added rather glumly.

"Hi, Nick. It's good to see you, son."

"You too, Dad."

"How's McKenzie?" Paul inquired, though not sure if he was doing the right thing by asking.

Nick didn't answer, tears welling up in his eyes instead. Then Lisa responded for him, "She's still critical, Paul. But she's hanging in there, and we're hopeful." Lisa's voice reflected the sadness she felt that her patient was still fighting for her life.

"You're hopeful!" Nick injected negatively, looking directly at his mother.

"Hope is sometimes all we have, son," Paul said, trying to allay his son's obvious frustration.

"Well, I'm just not feeling a whole lot of that right now. We don't even have a gun to protect ourselves."

"You don't need a gun, Nick."

"You had a gun in the Marines to protect yourself, didn't you! Don't you get it? Some of my friends were killed!

"I do get it, Nick," his father shot back. "But a gun is not the answer. You're too young yet."

"So much for your hope then," his son responded bitterly.

"I'm sorry, Nick. For the moment, please accept that my thoughts are with you and McKenzie. And they are hopeful."

Nick suddenly rose from his chair. "I need to get to the hospital."

"So soon?" Paul asked.

"Sorry, Dad. I'll call you during the week sometime."

"Okay, Nick. It's been good talking to you."

"You too. Bye, Dad. Bye, Mom." With that Nick was gone.

"Well, that went well," Lisa quipped. Then after several seconds of silence, she queried Paul a bit suspiciously. "So how are you?"

"I'm good. Things are good up here," Paul answered, nodding his head in a fairly nondescript fashion.

"That's a somewhat tepid response," Lisa said, picking up on Paul's hesitancy.

"We got a dog, Dad" Rianne said jubilantly.

"You did?" Paul exclaimed, his voice picking up some honest enthusiasm.

"His name is Ralph. He's a mutt, but I love him. We got him at the animal shelter. Come here, Ralphie." Rianne called the dog over while slapping the side of her leg. Ralph came and stood with his front paws on Rianne's legs, panting and smiling at the screen. Paul's heart nearly melted, and he could see how happy Rianne was with her newfound friend.

"He's cute, Paul," Lisa assured her husband. "You'll love him. He's part shepherd, part Lab, and only two years old. I think he'll be good for the kids."

"I'm sure," said Paul, pleased, but feeling like the odd man out. "How are things at the school, Rianne? Is anything getting back to normal?"

"Not really, Dad."

"One of the critically injured students passed away," Lisa explained. "It's tended to extend the mourning for obvious reasons." With that, several seconds of silence passed.

"Well, I sure wish you were all up here with me," Paul said, trying to recover the moment. "I'd love to show you around and cook you dinner."

"That'd be cool, Dad." Then Rianne went suddenly quiet, and Lisa knew what was on her mind.

"I think Ri has something she wants to ask you, Paul. She's been dying to."

"What's that, sweetheart?" Paul said, knowing full well what it was.

"Did you hear anything about my moon video?"

"Well, as a matter of fact, I did. And I can tell you that a lot of people are interested and looking into it, and at this point that's all I can say." Paul hoped his explanation would suffice.

"It's okay, Dad. I figured it was nothing. My feelings aren't hurt," the young girl said stoically.

Paul could sense his daughter's disappointment, but in this case it was probably better to leave it there. He couldn't risk telling her the truth, whatever that was. It would probably only scare her.

"I'll take Ralph outside and let you and Mom have some squishy time."

"Thanks, sweetheart. Appreciate it." Paul was proud of his daughter and felt his eyes well up a little as he watched Rianne leave the room with her dog.

Lisa waited until Rianne cleared the doorway and then asked with some concern, "Is there something you're not telling us, Paul?"

"Yes, there's something I'm not telling you, because at this point—I can't.

"Why?" she said with some futility, knowing the probable answer already.

"Because it's been classified. But between you and me, I will tell you this: our daughter may have found something really important. We just don't know for sure yet. For the moment, keep that to yourself. It's better that way for now."

The race to get back to the moon and onto Mars had been heating up substantially during the recent past. American private enterprise was picking up the slack for NASA in the new human space race. The United States still had prestige as the first country to put a man on the moon and held the lead in many areas of development, both human and unmanned, especially with the successes of NASA's Mars rovers and Space X, but other countries were gaining. The Russians, even though they were no longer giving Americans rides to the space station, still had a viable program worthy of respect. The Chinese were expanding a very competent system of their own, incorporating what appeared to be newly developed quantum-computing technology, and had set up a telescope array on the far side of the moon as well. India, Japan, and South Korea were also developing advanced projects and showing a lot of competence in unmanned missions. Orbiting the moon were satellites from multiple countries, but at the present moment, no country was remotely near pulling off another successful human moon mission.

For several years the United States, both governmental agencies and private entities, had been gearing up for such an event with plans to eventually launch Mars missions from the moon. With only 16.6 percent of the earth's gravity to contend with, moon launches would be far more cost-effective, as spacecraft could be built with a greater balance between essential equipment and propellant. Ice formations discovered at the moon's poles in limited quantities could be used to provide oxygen and hydrogen for human consumption and propellant. The dark side of the moon might harbor even more of the precious commodity. Solar winds were proposed as an effective deep-space propulsion mechanism. Mock-ups of various systems were being built by Galaxy Enterprises and others for testing, but there were many technical difficulties that would need to be resolved first, and that would take time.

In a meeting with NASA, Space X, and the consortium of companies that formed Galaxy Enterprises, it was determined that the most efficient and effective way to find out what was happening on the moon quickly, which when it came to space exploration was always a relative term, was to send an unmanned probe with the explicit task of identifying the heat source. Each unit had probes that they could adapt for such a mission, but in this regard NASA had the lead. Cost, normally a barrier, was regarded by the US government as less so in this instance: The situation had become acute. While optic telescopes on Earth had not seen any other signs of the initial anomaly, the airborne infrared telescopes and the JWST indicated that the energy output on the moon was increasing at an alarming rate, and it was determined that an orbital mission would take place first to get photographs (if possible) and collect any other available data. A follow-up rover-type landing would come next should the situation warrant.

Galaxy mission control kept Paul updated regarding the plan that was being formulated. Galaxy, Space X, and NASA would all be involved, but NASA would be taking the lead. They had more expertise in the areas this mission would involve, and it was a matter of national security. After receiving the new images taken from the ISS, NASA, which reports directly to the president, immediately contacted the Department of Defense, which was now monitoring the situation closely as well.

Paul had spent the day working with Martina, getting the Celestron telescope back to its original position in the ISS Destiny module. NASA felt they had gleaned all the useful information they were going to get from it and felt they needed to get it back to doing what it was designed to do—monitoring Earth. With global warming on the rise, extreme weather patterns were becoming a constant, and the big picture this eye-in-the-sky gave to those on the ground was invaluable.

Once the task was finished, Paul went to his crew quarters, what the astronauts called their CQs, to check his e-mails and perhaps make a call home. But it had been a busy day, and he decided to recharge with a short power nap. He asked Martina to wake him in half an hour.

Usually Paul had some difficulty falling asleep, even when it was for a normal nighttime duration. He occasionally considered using the sleeping aid provided to astronauts by Galaxy doctors, but he rarely did because he hated using medication. On this particular occasion, however, he could hardly keep his eyes open, and his thoughts began drifting as soon as he crawled into his sleeping bag. In short order he was sound asleep.

A half hour later, Martina returned to wake Paul, but after several minutes of standing outside his CQ and calling him with no response, she became alarmed. She didn't think it was a problem with the Seedra air-filtration system: the CO_2 level seemed to be just fine, or at least what all those onboard accepted as normal. Paul was probably just deep sleeping. She thought about just letting him sleep a little longer, but aware of his exacting nature and the pressure exerted by the Onboard Short Term Plan Viewer, which had everybody's daily tasks nailed down to the second, she thought it better that she not. With that she unzipped the flap to his cubical and looked in and tried to wake him once more with her voice. There was still no response.

"Paul," she said, shaking him gently. Still no response. Now she was getting really agitated. She tried once again, this time shaking him fairly hard, but nothing happened.

Martina and Paul were presently the only astronauts in the US section of the space station. Two more astronauts were scheduled to arrive in four weeks, one specifically to relieve Martina since she had already been at the station almost six months. There were two Russians onboard, but Martina was hesitant to ask for their help. Paul had been keeping her apprised of the situation on the moon, and at this point it was unclear if the Russians might actually be involved with what was going on up there. Normally politics were set aside at the space station. Everyone was too reliant on each other in so many ways that trust was paramount. But this situation had made for some awkwardness.

She tried one more time to wake Paul, but to no avail. She mulled over what to do next and then quickly propelled herself toward the Russian section of the ISS.

Anton Romanov was a seasoned space traveler with four missions under his belt going back to the late days of the Mir Space Station. He had seen people get sick on the International Space Station or sustain some minor injury, but there had never been a truly serious emergency that he could remember. Cosmonauts and astronauts were some of the healthiest people around because everyone knew that treating serious medical conditions was limited on the ISS. What was happening with Paul, however, seemed inexplicable, and that made it serious. Nothing Anton and Martina did was succeeding in reviving Paul. It was as though he had fallen into a coma.

Martina contacted Ken Ishida via the station's videoconferencing system while Anton went back to the Russian section and contacted his Russian mission-control counterpart. There were medical experts standing by on both sides of the planet, and hopefully one of the two teams would have a solution.

"You need to use your portable ultrasound," said Dr. Price, one of Galaxy's on-call physicians. "Check his head, chest, and abdomen and then download the information to us."

"And in the meantime?" asked Martina, wishing for something more immediate.

"I think it's probably best to monitor him for the time being until he wakes up on his own."

"And if he doesn't?" she persisted.

"Paul's health was excellent prior to launch. I am sure there is a logical explanation for what has happened. Perhaps a bump on the head while sleeping."

"We're tethered in when we sleep," Martina argued, frustrating the doctor somewhat.

"Perhaps something was floating around," he said, trying to reassure her.

"I didn't see anything."

"Let's just do the ultrasound and go from there, okay?" Price said with more than a hint of irritation.

"Okay," said Martina.

"Do you remember how to do it, or would you like me to stay with you online?" Price was actually being very understanding now.

"I remember, but I wouldn't mind your assistance. I'm a little shaken up by all this," the Italian admitted.

"Understandable. I'll wait while you get the machine."

Anton had returned to the US astronaut quarters a short time later, but the suggestions from the Russian team were about the same as those from the American side. They mentioned a few drugs the Russians had that might be of some use if Paul were on Earth and did not regain consciousness, but the drugs were not aboard the space station, and getting an unconscious man back to Earth for treatment would be risky at best.

Anton and Martina both knew how to use the portable ultrasound, but they were happy to have the doctor looking over their shoulder. So much training for astronauts and cosmonauts was for emergency situations, but to everyone's credit, they rarely arose. The consequence was that at times procedures could become a bit fuzzy, and the doctor's aid would help clarify the process. When they finished, they sent the data to the doctor and waited for a reply.

It was several hours before Dr. Price got back to them, and he was surprised to find out that Paul had still not regained consciousness.

"Where do we go from here?" asked Martina with deep concern for her crewmate.

"I am at a loss," said Price. "I am going to confer with colleagues down here and see if we can come up with an answer."

"Do you need us to run more tests or do another ultrasound?" Anton asked.

"I don't think that will help, Anton," replied Dr. Price. "The ultrasound you did was quite thorough, and what it told us is that Paul is healthy and none of this should be happening. I can't see that sleeping will hurt him, whereas waking him might have a negative effect, as in the case with sleepwalkers. I would just wait until we get back to you, probably tomorrow. With luck he will be awake by then, and all will be fine."

"But we still wouldn't know what caused it," Martina said, somewhat dismayed.

"One step at a time, Martina. Process of elimination is slow, but it's the best strategy we have at this point."

"Then we wait," Anton responded a bit grimly.

Paul had experienced flashes caused by cosmic rays when he closed his eyes to sleep onboard the ISS before, but nothing was ever as weird as what he was experiencing this time. He seemed to be dreaming, yet he wasn't sure he was asleep. It felt like he was leaving his body, like people who describe when they are being operated on and have a near-death experience where they are in the operating room, looking down at the doctors performing surgery. He opened his eyes a couple of times just to make sure he was in his sleeping bag and found that he was, but the feeling returned as soon as he closed his eyes again. The last time he did it, he fell into an immediate deep sleep with what seemed to be the most vivid dream imaginable.

Paul was not only having the dream, he found that he was trying to explain it to himself while it was occurring. He felt a sense of acceleration and exhilaration, but not a hint of fear. In fact, the experience was having a calming effect. He was comfortable, warm, and peaceful, and when he awoke, he felt rested, albeit in unfamiliar surroundings. Paul was standing in what appeared to be fog, which he was able to walk out of within a step or two, whereupon he found he was in an enclosed, though not unpleasant, space. It was clean and well lit without discernable walls, as if the fog was around only the periphery of the room behind which there were flat-panel fluorescent-like lights. Overhead he could see stars, and he suddenly realized that he was aware of gravity, though not nearly as strong as Earth's. While totally at ease, he was nonetheless convinced that this was one of the strangest dreams he had ever had. His level of awareness was so acute he felt it would be impossible for him to ever forget.

"And that would be fine," a voice said from out of the fog, except that Paul was unclear as to whether he had heard it or whether it was something happening strictly inside his head. Unsure, he decided to probe his own dream.

"Is someone there? Martina?"

"Martina is on the space station," was the answer he was sure he heard coming from strictly inside his head.

"And where am I?" asked Paul, amazed that he had developed schizophrenia so quickly, and not believing anything he was hearing at this point.

"You are here. And you are on the space station as well."

"How can that be?" Paul asked, almost laughing out loud. "And where is here?"

"This is a staging area."

"For what?" Paul asked, beginning to question whether he was actually asleep or not.

"For your indoctrination, or perhaps 'introduction' might be a better word."

"What am I being introduced to? And to whom or what am I speaking ?"

In nearly an instant, the fog disappeared, and Paul saw what appeared to be a woman in a white flowing gown, only it wasn't really a woman. But it was ephemeral and soothing and inviting. And beyond her were what appeared to be walls of glass or some type of force field, and past that, there was the dark backside of the moon's surface.

Paul approached her at the window-like barrier. He studied her intently, and she did nothing to stop him. He even reached out to touch her, but his hand went through her. It was as though she were a hologram, or a projection of some sort. But he could smell her, a fragrance similar to one that Lisa liked to wear, and she was beautiful. She was looking deep into his eyes, studying him, curious to learn as much about him as possible. And Paul sensed a warmth about her, as though she were a friend and he had nothing to fear.

After several moments, he asked, "Am I dreaming all this?"

"No," she answered, her mouth not moving.

"Then I must be hallucinating."

"Not that either," she responded, still without speaking.

"How can this be?" asked Paul. "Who are you?"

"All in due time, Paul."

"How do you know my name?"

"You told us," the entity acknowledged matter-of-factly.

"When? How?"

"With your thoughts."

"How? How can that be?"

"While we can communicate orally, exchanges between us and others are typically telepathic."

"And what is your name? What do you call yourself?" Paul asked, fully realizing that something other than dreams or hallucinations was going on here.

"We have no names in a formal sense. Recognition of whom we are communicating with is more deeply personal and identifiable than any name. Our name has never been central to the beings on the planets we have helped."

"What are you talking about? The planets you've helped?"

The entity became acutely aware that Paul had reached an emotional threshold and that attempting to digest any more information at this time would be counterproductive.

"I will answer all your questions in due time," the entity said, this time appearing to speak out loud. "But for now I think you need to return to your space station."

"How?" said Paul, somewhat indignantly.

"I will send you there."

"How? And how . . . when are you going to answer my questions?"

"When you come back," was the calm reply.

"When will that be?" he asked, somewhat adamantly.

"Whenever you would like. I trust you feel safe and relaxed?"

"I do," Paul responded, taking stock of his situation and realizing that he did feel safe and that there was little reason for attitude. In no way did he feel attacked or violated. "How will I get back? How will you know if I want to talk?"

"You can just tell us."

"Out loud?" Paul said in astonishment.

"Or just think it. However it happens, we'll know."

With that Paul woke up in his cubical onboard the ISS.

Martina was beside herself when Paul awoke. He was in good spirits but seemed unwilling to talk about what had happened, maintaining that it was nothing more than a very deep sleep. This explanation seemed to satisfy Anton who was still there with Martina and welcomed Paul back, adding "You gave us good scare," in his thick Russian accent.

Once Anton returned to the Russian section of the ISS, Martina probed a little deeper. "Are you all right?"

"I think so. In fact, I think I feel about as well as I have ever felt on this station."

"But what happened?" she asked, as if only an unequivocal explanation would give her any relief.

"I don't know. I don't know that anything happened. I think I want to go to sleep."

"Oh, don't say that. Please," Martina said with alarm. "Paul!"

But it was too late. Paul was already snoring.

When Paul woke the next day, he felt better than he had ever felt in his entire life, which was quite an extraordinary thing for an astronaut to feel. He exited his sleeping bag and used the WHC before joining Martina who was having some breakfast in Node 1. Paul could tell that Martina was watching him closely and hoping for an explanation as to what happened, but he was hesitant to say anything. After a full night's rest, he was on the verge of convincing himself it had all been a dream. But it had felt so real, unlike most dreams that often made no sense or were patchworks of people, places, and events both known and unknown. This one remained with him with every detail intact, every word spoken, and even the scent of what smelled like perfume the entity wore. He remembered the entity saying he could come back, just by thinking it. He wondered if that was true. His intuition told him that such a thought should scare him, and yet he felt no fear at all. If anything he felt excitement and anticipation, yet those feelings gave way to thinking it was all a dream once again.

"You're quiet," Martina probed gently.

"Just lost in thought," Paul offered.

"About yesterday, and what happened?"

"I don't know what happened, other than I fell asleep."

"You didn't just fall asleep, Paul. You fell off a cliff."

"Sorry."

"No need to feel sorry. But you must know that what happened is unusual and we ought to talk about it." The Italian was trying to be circumspect, but she had a duty as a fellow astronaut to watch out for his well-being.

"I don't know what to tell you. I went to sleep, and I had a dream, I think."

"What do you mean you think?"

"I don't know what to tell you right now, Martina. Maybe it's just too soon for me to sort it out. Maybe by tomorrow I will be able to make some sense of it all."

"That's fine," Martina said, not wanting to pressure him any further. She started to propel herself toward the lab and then latched onto a handhold and turned herself back to Paul. "Just let me know if there is anything I can do for you. You can count on me; you know that, right?"

"I know that," Paul responded, knowing it to be true.

When she left, he dove back into his thoughts to see if he could determine if it had all really happened, but he couldn't. Clearly time had passed for his crewmates while he was experiencing whatever it was he had experienced, and it had caused them considerable concern. Since he didn't want to subject them to any more alarm, he decided to test the entity's invitation to come back, but he would do so during his normal sleeping hours when, hopefully, no one would be the wiser.

"Station, Houston on Space to Ground One."

"Go ahead, Houston," Paul said, keying the mic.

"You gave us quite a scare. How are we this morning?" Ken Ishida was trying to sound cheerful but was clearly worried, not just about Paul, but the fate of the overall mission.

Once again Paul was unsure about what to say. Finally he responded, "I feel good. Honestly, never better. Guess I just needed some sleep."

"Well, Dr. Price is here with me, and I don't think that answer will satisfy him entirely," Ken said.

"That's right, Paul. Dr. Price here. I want you to take blood samples and urine samples so we can analyze them and possibly nail this thing down for future reference. Of course we'll have to wait until we get them back down to Earth. In the meantime I'd like for Martina to do another ultrasound just to see if we missed anything yesterday. Any questions?"

"No, sir," Paul said a little too smartly. He hated poking himself with needles. Maybe Martina could help with that too.

"He sounded perfectly normal," Dr. Price noted after they ended the communication on the Houston end.

"I agree," said Ken. "But my intuition is nagging at me for a better answer."

"I don't think the ultrasound is going to reveal much more than we know already," the doctor admitted. "What I would really like to do is an MRI, but that's not possible. I think the best we can do at this point is wait and see and support."

"This does not make me happy," Ken said resignedly.

"Me either," responded the doc.

That night prior to falling asleep, Paul found himself thinking about his previous encounter with the entity and events that might happen next. And though he felt anticipation, intellectual curiosity, and even friendship, he found himself wrestling with the notion that he should feel afraid of doing what he was about to do. If the entity he spoke with was truly real, was it also truly benevolent? Or was this just a ruse to suck him in? It felt like he was at war with his own brain, and to that extent it felt silly since he still didn't know if any of it was real. But there was only one way to find out, and so, disregarding his better judgment, he decided to take the plunge and specifically thought about going back. With that he fell asleep.

Paul quickly found himself back in the same space he had been the first time. This time he slowly tried to penetrate the fog further, expecting there to be a window within a few feet, but he simply got lost in the cloud and actually felt a moment of panic.

"Are you there?" he called out, his voice a little shaky.

With that the fog began to slowly dissipate, and Paul found himself within a structure that was forming around him, a large, ornate, space-age cathedral-like edifice. Paul felt like he was in a protective bubble of some sort as the structure built rapidly from the base to its top. Magnificent when completed, its walls were solid but paper thin, with a bluish-green light emanating from the material itself, giving the entire structure an ephemeral glow. It was cavernous inside yet comfortable and welcoming. It smelled fresh, like springtime, and there were sounds that reminded him of nature but that were totally unrecognizable and yet soothing and reassuring.

"Peaceful, don't you think?"

Paul wasn't sure he had heard a voice or whether it was all in his head. No matter, he turned and saw the entity he had spent time with before, standing behind him.

"Do you like it?"

"What is this place?" Paul said out loud, feeling funny having noticed that once again the entity's lips had not moved.

"It is one of my favorite places when we travel," the entity responded. "It reminds me of something I might call home."

"And where would that be?" Paul asked, finally feeling like he was getting somewhere.

"We are not quite sure anymore. We are only aware of the last hundred or so."

"Homes?" Paul said, not able to hide his shock at such an idea.

"Yes," the entity replied.

"That's nuts!" Paul blurted out, which elicited an out-loud verbal laugh from the entity.

"Hopefully your species will know what that feels like in the future."

"Why would we want to know that?" Paul said, starting to feel a little uneasy.

"Because it means you would have survived long enough to outlive Earth."

"Where are we now," Paul demanded, "or am I just hallucinating all this?"

Suddenly the cathedral-like structure dematerialized as the glass-like room he had been in previously rematerialized. Outside was the barren landscape of the moon.

"We are on the backside of your moon."

"I see," said Paul, now certain that he was indeed experiencing something real.

"So you're taking up residence here? Why not on the earth itself? It's really much nicer," he said a little testily.

"We have no desire to stay here permanently. Just for as long as we are needed."

"For what?"

"To get you on your feet."

"I don't understand," said Paul. "I always thought we were already on our feet." He felt frustrated because he wasn't able to put this all together, but once again he noted that he felt no fear. He was getting frightening information from an alien of some sort, yet he was feeling like he was having a perfectly normal conversation. He also became aware that the entity looked a lot like Lisa, his wife.

"Please tell me what's happening?" He waited a moment. "Please. Who are you? What are you doing here? Are you some kind of advanced civilization or ancient race, or what?"

"To call us an ancient race would be a kind of misnomer. While we have been around for a long time, as you conceive of it, time has ceased having much meaning for us."

"How so?" Paul probed.

"Because we have learned how to traverse the vastness of space at near light speed, explore other galaxies, and exploit the paradoxes of black holes to locate other habitable universes. Our lives are typically thousands of times longer than yours. The problem is that for all the life we've found throughout all the places we've explored, we have discovered that intelligent life is somewhat rare overall and often in danger of extinguishing itself. Thus we see it as our mission to locate and help species that struggle to overcome things we overcame many millions of your years before."

"And what's my part in all this?" Why me?" Paul asked, somewhat intrigued.

"We're not sure," the entity communicated honestly, clearly hinting that they were still assessing Paul. "We are looking for an emissary to communicate with your planet for us. There are many reasons in your favor, and we are trying to determine if you would be our best choice."

"Why do you need someone to do that? You seem to be communicating with me pretty well on your own here."

"But you would be familiar to the people on Earth. If *you* could learn to trust us, perhaps the world could learn to trust us as well."

"Doubtful," Paul said. Then he added, "Just trying to be honest."

"We understand. But it is worth a try. Earth's future may depend on it."

"That sounds ominous."

"It is, but we are–hopeful." With that word Paul's mind flashed back to the conversation he had had with his son as the entity continued. "We have been able to save many planets just like yours."

"Save them from what?"

"Themselves."

Without warning Paul found himself back in his CQ sleeping bag. Only this time he was wide awake and felt like he was functioning at 100 percent. He also felt as though he had no idea as to what was really happening—yet, but the entity had certainly given him a lot to think about.

Though Paul felt physically well, he also had a desperate desire to talk to Lisa. He was not at a point where he felt he could share this experience he was having with anyone but Lisa. He trusted her opinion, both as his wife and as a doctor. He knew she would let him know if what he was going through was really happening or whether he was suffering from a mental illness. Perhaps this was all being brought on by his being in space. The thought saddened him, as he was proud of being an astronaut and worried that all his dreams would come crashing down as a result.

He wanted to call Lisa, but it dawned on him that there might not be a secure way to do it: Galaxy and NASA would be nosey after his big sleep. He found himself feeling a bit paranoid that someone would overhear or intercept his communication no matter how he did it. He could call on his cell phone, but the signal was bouncing off satellites. He could wait until the weekend when he was scheduled for a videoconference with his family, but again, it might not be secure. He was also concerned that Rianne might hear some of the conversation, and that could be disastrous. A youngster could not be expected to understand the implications of what might actually be happening and keep the information to herself. Paul didn't even understand the implications.

Paul tried to think if there was anyone else he could bounce this off, but he couldn't. The communication problems would be the same, and there was no one who could replace Lisa for him. He thought about telling Martina, but while they had an excellent working relationship, he couldn't count on how she might react to what he had to tell her. She was from another country, and English was a second language, which might present gaps in her understanding. On top of that, she would be leaving in less than two weeks, and if she thought Paul was going crazy, she would very quickly have an opportunity to tell those on the ground. No. It was better to keep this to himself, but it was killing him.

"They didn't find anything unusual," Paul told his wife the next day. He had decided not to tell Lisa about the dreams, or whatever they were, but there was no reason he couldn't discuss going to sleep the way he did.

"You say they did an ultrasound?" she said, all doctor now.

"Two of them. Martina did the second one yesterday, but like I said, they didn't find anything that could explain it."

"An MRI would be better, or an fMRI. The ultrasound is very limited with hard heads."

"Are you calling me a hard head?" Paul asked kiddingly, thinking she was dissing his personality.

"Maybe a little," she teased back. "I was thinking more along the lines that ultrasounds are more useful with babies because their skulls are still soft. Yours isn't!

"I would give anything if we could have some privacy. Just for a few minutes," Paul said plaintively.

"Normally I would think you were trying to be funny or maybe even romantic. But I'm a little concerned about what I'm hearing."

"How so?" Paul said quizzically.

"I'm not sure. But I know Rianne always talks about how calm and steady you are, but you don't sound calm and steady to me right now. That is different."

"Sorry," Paul offered apologetically. "I don't want you to worry."

"Does this have anything to do with your classified information? Anything we should be worried about?"

"I don't think so. But the point is I can't talk about it."

"What does NASA say, if I might ask?" Lisa was trying to help Paul solve his dilemma more than merely fishing for information.

"That's the problem. I don't know what to tell them either. I've probably said too much already."

"So when you asked for privacy, it wasn't my body you wanted, just my mind?"

"I wouldn't say that. I've always been good at multitasking," he joked. "But I tell you I have always found your mind to be the sexiest thing about you."

"You're a flatterer. And I love you. And by the way, my patient is still in critical condition, but I promised her that when she pulled through, she could meet you."

"That would be my pleasure. I'd love it," Paul responded enthusiastically.

"And I love you, Paul. You take care of yourself, and call me if you need to."

"I'll call even if I don't," he answered with affection.

"Bye," she whispered softly, and with that ended the call.

While it had been satisfying to talk to her, Paul realized his problem had not abated. But he didn't know what he would do next.

Rianne had been playing outside with friends when Paul's call had come through, and for that Lisa was grateful. She knew how important these calls were to Rianne, but in an effort to be fair to her, Lisa was often unfair to herself. Eighteen months was a long time to be away from your spouse, and she relished having a moment that they could spend together and flirt. It wasn't as good as sex, but it was the best that they would get for some time, and she was grateful that it happened in such a way that she didn't even need to feel guilty. But she also felt sad and worried. Sad that she couldn't really help, and worried because she still didn't know what the real issue was. What she did figure out was that Paul was now keeping new information from NASA that related to information that NASA and the DOD had already classified as top secret from the public. Whatever was going on was putting a lot of pressure on Paul if he didn't even feel he could talk to his superiors or crewmates about it. In that regard she felt totally helpless and could understand how he probably felt the same.

That night was Friday, and as they always did, the crews aboard the ISS shared a meal together. Martina contributed some special treats she had brought with her from Italy. She had been saving them since she arrived at the ISS, and with her stay winding down, she felt that it was time to break out the polenta, cannoli, and risotto. While freeze-dried food brought back to life with boiling water was not nearly as good as freshly made honest-to-goodness Italian food, it was a treat nonetheless. Cosmonauts and astronauts alike enjoyed the delicacies, particularly the cute little servings of Chianti, which Martina managed to smuggle onboard.

After dinner Martina and Paul went back to the US section and got ready for sleep. Paul liked her a lot and thought that if he hadn't known Lisa, he might have tried to get to know Martina when he returned to Earth. It was a silly thing to even think about since he was perfectly happy with Lisa, and Martina was married, but it was impossible not to fantasize about such things on a mission of such long duration. Quarters were close, and privacy minimal, and there was no choice in the matter: You got to know your space partners very well. Beyond that, everything was off limits. Still, he knew he would miss her when she left, and he wished he could talk to her in confidence, but the stakes were too high, so he excised the thought from his mind.

That night Paul fell asleep in what seemed like a normal way, but he once again awoke in the room that the entity claimed was on the moon. Once again it was shrouded in fog. Paul was only there a minute or two when he heard a familiar voice. As he stood there, a shape emerged from the cloud, and standing in front of Paul was Lisa, or someone who appeared to be her.

"Where am I, Paul," she said, unsure but steady.

"The moon, I think," he said, still not sure if he was really talking to her or dreaming.

Lisa walked toward him and touched his face. Her hand felt real, and he wanted so badly to hold her in his arms but was uncertain. Not knowing if this was all real, or if he was being duped, or if he perhaps was sick, he chose to keep his distance. But if someone were reading his mind, that person was doing a pretty good job of it. He was also dealing with a sense of guilt. Part of the mission was about being away from family and friends for a sustained period of time, and it was impossible not to feel as though he were cheating. Yet in his mind he knew he was not asking for any of this; it was just happening.

"Is this what you wanted to talk to me about?" Lisa seemed to understand intuitively what was going on.

"You don't think I'm dreaming all this?" he said, almost childlike, looking for some adult to offer him guidance.

"If you are, we both are," Lisa said, seeming sure of her own observations.

"How can you tell?" Paul asked. "What makes you seem so sure?"

"I just know," she responded. "And I don't mean to be flip, but I am not afraid. My intuition tells me that this is real and I should be scared out of my wits, but I'm not. Whatever is happening here is not frightening, and I trust it. Is that what you were trying to find out? Is that what you wanted to ask me when you called?"

Paul was overwhelmed and took Lisa in his arms and kissed her. He held her for several seconds and then looked at her face.

"I love you," he said with deep affection.

"I know," said Lisa. "And I appreciate whoever is responsible for giving us this opportunity."

He kissed her again and then straightaway woke up back in his space-station quarters, once again alone and confused. Still feeling groggy, he fell back into a deep and restful sleep. Sometime later the ringtone on his cell phone woke him with a start. It was Lisa.

"Paul?" She sounded excited.

"Yes," he said, unsure of how he should respond to his own wife.

"I understand, Paul. Everything. I think you should trust your gut and see what they have to say. I love you."

"Are you feeling all right?" he asked cautiously.

"Never better, Paul. You know that. See you in my dreams."

With that the call ended, and now Paul was sure this was the real deal.

"What do you make of his condition?" asked Dr. Price of Martina via videoconference.

Ken Ishida, Dr. Price, and a whole host of other doctors and psychologists had been discussing Paul's condition and reactions for a good portion of the day. What they were concerned about was not that anything was wrong but that there wasn't. It's pretty much a fact that everyone has *something* wrong with him or her. Everyone has something in his or her DNA that could cause a problem down the road, or something inconsequential to spaceflight that can still become a problem, such as a tooth cavity. But the ultrasound that Martina did revealed that even things that were known to exist prior to Paul's departure had disappeared, and that was a mystery. It was as though his time in outer space was having the opposite effect that long-duration missions have had on other astronauts. Paul was suddenly getting healthier. All his vital signs had actually gotten stronger, at least ever since his long sleep.

"Paul appears to be fine," said Martina. "He seems a little worried on occasion, but perhaps that's because we keep watching him like he's a lab rat. But I can tell you that his sense of humor is intact, and his concentration when we are working together is exceptional. Overall, I think he is doing fine, if not better, for the ordeal."

"Well, that's reassuring to hear," said Dr. Price, "but I am going to want you to continue collecting blood samples and urine samples daily to bring back with you. And I want you to keep taking ultrasounds every two days until your departure."

"What do I tell Paul?" she said, certain that he would object or become suspicious.

"Tell him it's routine," said Ishida. "Tell him that this is a long-duration flight and we have to investigate everything new associated with it. And this is new."

"Understood," said Martina.

"Just keep an eye on him," said Dr. Price.

"No problem," answered the Italian. "He's my friend."

It was becoming clear to Paul that he needed to have a frank conversation with his superiors about what had been happening to him. But whom to talk to? The problem was he didn't have enough information from the entity and therefore could not be clear about what he was communicating. He could talk to officials from Galaxy Enterprises, but they were a private enterprise and did not represent the government per se, and this would certainly be considered a national-security issue, if not a world-security issue. He could talk to NASA, but NASA reported directly to the president, and Paul knew the president had already communicated with the Department of Defense about the anomaly Rianne had discovered. That's what led to the find being classified. He wondered what their reaction would be with this additional information. He felt certain that the DOD would take an offensive posture, and that concerned him. Up to this point, his experience with the aliens (if that was what they were: he was still wrestling with his doubts) felt totally benign. In fact, it surprised him that he was feeling somewhat protective of them. In that regard he was already functioning as emissary.

But time was of the essence since preparations on Earth were underway to launch a probe to the moon. It would be an expensive mission, and Paul felt he already had some of the answers they were looking for and felt like he might be able to get more. But would they believe him? He worried that everyone was going to think he was crazy, and that would end his career in space, but he didn't feel he could let such thoughts stop him. He had to risk it, and it almost seemed like it was something the aliens were hoping he would do. They were leaving the move up to him, and the aliens had so much invested in their relationship with him by now that he found it hard to believe they would abandon him in his efforts. He decided that the next day he would have a videoconference with Galaxy and NASA and bring them up to speed on what he knew. He fell asleep that night with a clear sense of purpose and a bit of relief.

In the morning Paul awoke and saw that the Onboard Short Term Plan Viewer already had a full day of activities lined up for him. Some were critical maintenance items, while others were things that could wait, and not nearly as important as what he needed to discuss. He climbed out of his sleeping bag, and after reprioritizing the day, he called mission control and arranged an afternoon meeting. Then he called Lisa.

"Is this a good time?" he asked her, his voice sounding a little nervous.

"I'm at the hospital, but I can spare a few minutes. Are you okay?"

"I've arranged a videoconference for this afternoon. I'm going to talk to Galaxy and NASA about, you know, what's been happening." He was being careful, knowing the calls were probably monitored.

"Are you sure that's a good idea?"

"No. But I'm obligated to say something, and sooner rather than later."

"I would agree, Paul. It's a judgment call, and I trust yours."

"I just wanted you to know because it might affect my career—and both our lives. It all sounds so crazy."

"But it's not, and you know it!" Lisa said, trying to bolster him for the ordeal ahead.

"But it could be a dream. Or a delusion. Maybe I *am* sick. You know how anal NASA and Galaxy can be about psychological evals."

"Yes. But it doesn't apply in this case. Whatever it is, it's something we both experienced. And I, for one, am *not* crazy, nor in space. In fact, I just performed a very difficult surgery. And I say you're not crazy either. So just hold that thought."

Paul laughed, admiring her logic. "I'll do that. At least I'll try. I'll see if I can sneak a call tonight. Let you know how it goes."

"Paul," she hesitated for a moment, "good luck." Lisa ended the call, fully aware of what a difficult position Paul was in but fully confident in his good judgment and his heart.

Several of the tasks Paul completed that day took longer than expected, but he managed to finish everything on his list before the meeting. He had been mulling over how he would start the conversation all morning, but when the videoconference actually started, all his planning seemed to fall by the wayside.

Ken Ishida, Dr. Price, John Wilner, Julian Ames, and Teddy Brower were conferencing from Galaxy, with Eric Holtz and Jerry Gomez, representatives from NASA, also joining them. Holtz was NASA's deputy director of operations, and Gomez was the lead scientist heading up the emergency probe mission to the moon. Both Holtz and Gomez seemed like they had better things to do than speak with a space-station astronaut who was sleeping a lot, and their attitude seemed a little detached right from the start. Paul knew them both, though not well, but decided not to let himself be intimidated. Ken Ishida started the meeting.

"You called a conference, Paul, and we assumed it was about what you've experienced in regard to your sleep patterns. Is that right?"

"In a way, yes."

"In a way?" Ken asked, waiting for clarification.

"It's difficult to know where to start."

"Do you need to come home, Paul?" Dr. Price interjected abruptly.

"Not at all, Doctor. I need to explain. I wasn't asleep." For all his planning, Paul simply found himself diving in. There was no looking back now.

"Then what were you doing?" Eric Holtz asked, seemingly irritated by the whole conversation.

"I was on the moon," Paul shot back.

Paul's comment resulted in a moment of total silence. Several heads dropped and looked at the floor, seemingly resigned to the fact that their astronaut had gone bonkers and that the current ISS mission was disintegrating in front of their eyes. Finally Ken's eyes came back up to the screen.

"Do you want to explain?" he said guardedly.

"I can't. At least not yet. I don't have enough information."

"Then on what basis, are you saying all this? I don't understand," was Gomez's reaction.

"Paul, why don't you just tell us what you know and let us take it from there." Ken was trying as best as he could to remove the tension in this virtual room and make it easier on Paul. But in the back of Ken's mind, he was convinced that Paul was in deep psychological trouble.

"I'm aware of just how insane all of this is going to sound, but I needed to tell you now because I think I can get all the information you need without a mission to the moon."

"How?" Ken asked, some small amount of faith in his astronaut returning.

"There is an entity on the moon. Or entities. I don't know yet because I've only spoken with one so far."

"When did this happen?" Dr. Price questioned, less interested in the answer than what it might reveal about Paul's state of mind.

"The day none of my crewmates could wake me."

"Why didn't you say anything then?" asked a perturbed Eric Holtz.

"Because I thought it must have been a crazy dream. Then it happened again, and certain things occurred that made me suspect that it was real."

"Like what?" Ken asked, looking for specifics.

"I remembered every detail. My senses were hyperactive. The entity was communicating with me telepathically."

"Oh, come on now," Holtz almost snorted.

"She also spoke to me directly, out loud," Paul persisted.

"She?" asked Ken.

"I think. I don't know if she was real."

"Now I am truly confused," said Ken.

"She seemed more like a projection, or a hologram. I reached out to touch her, but my hand went through her. But I could smell her. And I felt no fear. None whatsoever."

"What did she want?" John Wilner asked, intrigued by what he was hearing. He had known Paul for a long time and trusted him implicitly.

"She still hasn't told me."

"Have you seen her more than once?" Julian Ames inquired.

"Yes. Two times now. As near as I can tell, they are assessing whether they can trust me."

"For what?" asked Holtz.

"I think they want me to speak for them," said Paul. "I think they're going to do something. I just don't know what it is."

Holtz looked at Ken Ishida and said, "This isn't good. If he's telling the truth or if he isn't. We've got a problem either way."

"When you were on the moon, were you on the surface, Paul?" Wilner queried. "Were you in a spacesuit?"

"No. I was dressed as I am now. I was in a room of sorts. And once I was in a huge, beautiful structure. But when I asked a question, the structure disappeared, and I was back in the room. And beyond was the moon. The surface of the moon."

Paul thought of bringing up his encounter with Lisa, but he found himself reluctant to drag her into what seemed like such a ludicrous-sounding story.

Teddy Brower was the youngest of the group and probably the most open. Not one to speak very often, he raised his hand like he was back in school.

"Yes, Ted," Ken said, encouraging him to join the conversation.

"You say you saw this entity two times. Are you still in touch? Can you communicate with it?"

"Yes," Paul responded. "Whenever I'd like."

"How?" asked Ken.

"All I have to do is think it or say it. It seems my body goes into a deep sleep, and I end up there."

"Could you go there right now?" Holtz asked, almost sneering.

"I don't think it works like that, nor do I think they would let that occur. At least not yet."

"So you're just a special case? It's just a personal experience?" Holtz was getting very sarcastic now.

"As I said, I don't have enough information yet to make a determination about who they are or what their true intent is. I can only tell you what I know." Paul was unsure how they were taking all this. Somewhere in the back of his mind, he was certain they were going to get him off the station ASAP.

After a long, painful silence, Ken Ishida grabbed the conversational reigns. "Paul, you've given us all a lot to digest, and it hasn't been easy. I want to confer with my colleagues down here, and then we'll get back to you."

"I understand," said Paul, a little downtrodden.

Ken continued, "Please understand that we're not doubting what you experienced, but we need to determine if it's our reality or just yours. I'm sure you understand."

"I do, sir. I have been having the same arguments with myself."

"Well, that's a good sign," Ken said warmly. "I want you to take some time to yourself the rest of the day and try not to think about it."

"And don't try to contact this entity in any way for the time being," Dr. Price interjected.

"I second that," said Ken. "Let us talk about it and all get on the same page before we move forward. Understood?"

"Yes, sir."

With no further fanfare, Paul's screen went to the Galaxy logo. He didn't know if he had done well stating his case or whether he had just blown his entire career. One way or the other, he knew it was going to be a long night.

Ken Ishida remained neutral, while Wilner, Ames, and Brower put some stock in what Paul had told them. They had all worked with Paul for several years and knew he was poised under fire. If he seemed unsure of things right now, there was probably good reason, but they had faith in his ability to cope. If something strange was going on, there wasn't a more stable person to be dealing with it than Paul as far as they were concerned.

Eric Holtz and Jerry Gomez had softened a little. As farfetched as it all sounded, there was no denying that something was happening on the far side of the moon that defied explanation, and the coincidence of Paul's stated experience was hard to ignore. As was the fact, which Dr. Price brought up, that something was making Paul healthier, which in itself was odd. Ironically, it was the youngest among them who broke the impasse.

"I don't think we have anything to lose. I think we should encourage Paul to continue making contact and see if he can get any answers." When he finished speaking, Teddy gave one emphatic nod of his head as if to say there was nothing else to discuss about the matter.

"But if he is taking us down a blind path, then what?" Holtz still sounded totally unconvinced.

"Let's cover our bases," Gomez offered, "because one thing is certain. Something is going on up there, and we need to get information. Personally I don't care where it comes from. Let's keep planning on launching the probe *and* work with Paul."

Ken Ishida knew Lisa Franklin-Connors longer than he had known Paul Connors. She was a noted cardiothoracic surgeon who had once saved Ken's wife's life after a horrendous car crash. Later Ken and his wife got to know Lisa even better after Paul joined Galaxy's space program, so on this particular night, Ken felt perfectly comfortable calling Lisa, nor was it unusual for him to do so. On missions of long duration, he felt it was his duty to stay in touch with the astronauts' families on Earth, but where such calls were sometimes awkward, with Lisa it was a pleasure. She was Southern, gentile, and incredibly intelligent, and speaking with her was always easy. However, his reason for calling this particular evening had more to do with her professional opinion, and Ken was hoping she could remain objective: her husband's life might depend on it. As a doctor her input could be invaluable in sorting out the dilemma the space program now found itself in—whether to trust her husband's sanity.

"I was informed that Paul called you this morning about the videoconference he scheduled for today," Ken stated right off.

"So you've been spying on us?" Lisa mused. While Lisa and Paul had always suspected that their communications might be monitored, actually being told it was so made her surprisingly testy. "Don't you need a warrant or something for that?"

"Lisa . . ."

"How long has that been going on?" she asked with slightly feigned irritation.

"Just today."

"Why am I having trouble believing that?"

"We felt it was imperative, and a decision had to be made right away. In the interests of national security, there just wasn't time to see a judge."

"I see. So you, the company, and the government just step on our privacy? Nice."

"Do you know what the meeting today was about?" he inquired, trying to persuade her to tell him what she knew rather than revealing his own hand.

"Your people listened to the call. Why don't you ask them?"

"Lisa, please," Ken pleaded.

"I have a good idea," she responded.

"And could you tell me what that is?"

While Lisa trusted Ken, she knew she needed to be careful for Paul's sake. The government was not kind when it came to divulging classified information.

"I know it was about the anomaly that our daughter, Rianne, was first to spot on the moon." That seemed perfectly safe to say.

"Go on."

"And about the dreams Paul's been having," she continued.

"He told you?"

"Yes."

"And you think they're dreams?"

"No. I don't," she said emphatically.

"On what do you base that opinion?"

"Personal experience."

"How so?" he asked, intrigued by her response.

Lisa turned the tables. "Have you been monitoring *all* our communications?"

Ken's first instinct was to lie, but since he was looking for the truth from her, he came to the decision that he needed to speak the truth as well. "Yes," he answered, "most of them."

"And did any of the people in your company who monitor our calls and videoconferences ever mention to you that we had talked about those dreams?"

"No. Not specifically. They said there were some cryptic comments on occasions, but we just assumed they were the kind of private form of communication that most couples engage in. We didn't ascribe anything specific to them beyond that."

"Then ask me a question?"

"What do you mean?" Ken asked, feeling suddenly cornered.

"Ask me a question about what Paul told you today. About what happened. Or where. Or the experience itself."

Ken understood immediately where she was headed and decided to cut to the chase. "Why don't you just tell me what you know?"

"I know there's an entity on the moon. I know it has been communicating with Paul. I know that it wants him to do something but hasn't said what that is specifically. And I know it's real because it brought me there so Paul and I could talk about it privately because they knew you were listening. Whoever it is, whatever it is, knows exactly what we're thinking.

"Anything else you can tell me?"

"That's already a lot. Additionally, it was a beautiful experience. I felt totally peaceful and unafraid."

"Did you meet this entity?"

"No. Just Paul. We talked, he hugged me, and when I woke up back at our house, I called him and told him I understood.

I told him he should trust his gut. Of course you knew that because you were probably listening."

"Yes. We were," Ken admitted. "And you don't think it could all have been a dream?"

"Oh, come on, Ken. Do you think we both just happened to experience the same dream and I just happened to call him from Earth to tell him?" Lisa was adamant, but Ken seemed to understand.

"Aren't you worried about all this?" he asked her, sounding totally perplexed.

"Yes, I am," Lisa responded. "But not about the alien, or aliens, or whatever that is about, but what the folks on Earth are going to do about it. That's my real concern here."

"You don't think you're being a little Pollyannaish about it?" he said, chastising her a little.

"I wish you could have been there. I have never felt a sense of peace as strong as what I felt that night. I imagine if there is a heaven, that's what it will feel like."

"That's a pretty strong endorsement."

"My strongest." She thought for a moment and said, "I hope Paul's career doesn't suffer for this. He's really had no choice in the matter, and neither did I. It all just happened."

"Why you and Paul?" Ken asked, trying to make sense of it all.

"That I can't tell you. I suspect we'll find out at some point. There's usually a reason for everything."

"I appreciate your talking with me, Lisa. I will try to keep this between us."

"I don't believe that for a second, Ken. But I'm not worried about it. If my being on the hot seat can help protect Paul, I'm willing to take my chances. I tell you he's not crazy, and you can tell anybody who asks that I said so!"

"I'll do that." Ken ended the call, confused, empowered, and saddened that he may have lost a dear friend.

"We want you to make contact again," Ken told Paul the next day. "We want you to get as much information as you can, with a priority on your safety, of course."

"Of course," said Paul, "but I don't think there is any danger."

"We wish we could do an fMRI on you while you did this," interjected Dr. Price. "But there is no way that can be done on the space station."

"I guess you'll just have to trust me."

"I guess," the doctor quipped.

Ken went on, "We have a list of questions we are sending you to ask this entity, in addition to questions you may ask on your own."

"Thanks," said Paul. I appreciate any help I can get."

"When do you plan on doing this?" Ken asked, hoping it would be soon.

"Tonight. Maybe sooner. I feel a bit of relief now that you're all in the loop. What convinced you to do this, if I might ask?"

"Your colleagues were very supportive of you," Ken said. "And your wife was very convincing as well."

"You talked to Lisa?" Paul said, a little surprised.

"I did," Ken responded. "She could have been a lawyer instead of a doctor, though I'm personally grateful she isn't."

"What did she tell you?"

"She told me some of the same things you told me at our meeting, and since we had been monitoring your communications, it was hard to deny the validity of what she said. She also told me that you weren't crazy!"

"Let's hope she's right." Paul said only half joking.

"Paul," Dr. Price broke in, "we're limited in what we can monitor under the circumstances, but I am going to have Martina take the electrocardiogram pack out and hook you up. It won't tell us everything we want to know, but at least we'll be able to track your vitals."

Martina, who had just floated into the node as Dr. Price was talking, indicated she understood the request with a nod of her head, as did Paul.

"There is probably no need for me to say this, Paul," said Ken, "but keep us apprised. And be careful."

"Copy that," said Paul. The conference ended, and after the Galaxy logo appeared on his screen, he repeated what he had just said, only this time as a warning to himself. "Copy that. Be careful."

"What's going on?" Martina inquired, having come to the conversation late.

"Nothing much," Paul answered. "I think mission control wants to make sure we can follow instructions."

"Typical," Martina laughed, though not fully buying into Paul's explanation. Martina then went to get the electrocardiogram kit, and Paul took his shirt off so that she could attach the electrodes. Up until this point, he hadn't felt any fear. But now that everyone who should know, knew, he felt uncomfortable and found himself questioning his own allegiance. Was it to an entity that he had known for only a short while, but who, up until now, appeared to pose no threat? Or was it to everyone on Earth, many of whom would surely be afraid and would undoubtedly try to protect themselves and their families as a result. In mulling these questions over, Paul began to grasp the complexity, perils, and far-reaching consequences of what the aliens were asking of him.

As Paul waited for Martina's return he surprised himself as he spoke out loud, "Lord, I'm sorry I don't talk to you often, but I'm in a quandary over my allegiance to the people of Earth, and their right to protect their loved ones, and a being who I hardly know but am convinced poses no threat and could help mankind in unimaginable ways. If you have any thoughts, Lord, I'm open to your suggestions 24/7. Amen."

Something inexplicable was also happening on the planet's surface that at first went unnoticed, but as the phenomenon gained momentum over a period of weeks and the news media suddenly caught on, it escalated quickly into a major crisis. A rash of thefts were being reported, not just in the United States, but around the globe, and the thefts seemed to be targeted. Guns were disappearing, but in a very geographically random fashion with no apparent rhyme or reason. There were reports of guns missing from private homes, gun lockers, and stores, and in a majority of cases, there was no trace or clue. Military weapons appeared not to be targeted, nor were law enforcement's. At least not yet. Authorities were baffled.

Paul was busy making mental notes during his next excursion to the moon. Once there, he concentrated on the details of his surroundings as well as imprinting the clues his senses were imparting to him. He noted that the electrodes that Martina had placed on him were no longer there, but he assumed that since his actual body was still on the ISS, it only made sense that the electrodes would be there too. The same was true for his cell phone, which would have come in handy at a time like this for recording notes. How were they doing all this? he wondered.

On this outing Paul found himself in the cathedral-like structure again, but being alone, at least for the moment, he had an opportunity to observe it more freely. The central area was like an arboretum of sorts, with a few exotic trees, which were totally unfamiliar to him, as well as bird-like creatures that chirped and flitted, creating the most wonderful sounds so pleasant to hear for someone deprived of real nature for the past two months. Paul had a few environmental recordings in his CQ to remind him of Earth, but none of those compared to what he was experiencing at this moment.

The building had windows of a sort, or force fields, through which Paul could view the moon's landscape. It was barren, austere, and jagged, but its cold isolation had a beauty all its own. Inside he saw a few of what appeared to be entryways, marked by curtains of light created by thousands of pretty blue laser-like beams. But since he did not know how they worked, nor what lie beyond, he decided not to try going through them. He had yet to determine whether he could feel pain, or sustain physical injury, or whether he was totally immune from such things in his present state.

Aside from the creatures in the center arboretum, Paul saw no other signs of life as he continued exploring the structure's interior. But his senses told him he was not alone, and he once again noted a feeling of tranquility washing over him. He was positive he was actually on the moon, or at least some part of his consciousness was, yet he knew without a doubt that he was in no danger. Enjoying the moment he turned around to explore in another direction and saw the entity a short distance away, patiently waiting and watching.

"Hi," he said to the entity while raising his hand and waving, immediately feeling kind of ridiculous about his seeming informality, but not knowing exactly how to approach the situation.

"Hello," the entity communicated with a smile, but without speaking out loud. "I believe we have much to discuss. Much that you want to know."

"It's like you're reading my mind," Paul said aloud.

"I am," the entity communicated. "Not that a good guess would not suffice in this instance."

"So what's the first thing I want to know?" he asked, curious as to whether the alien could really figure it out.

"You feel uncomfortable because you don't know what to call me besides 'the entity.' But 'entity' actually sounds like a nice name to me."

"That works," said Paul, laughing. "And you're right. That's what I was thinking. And 'entity' is a fine name for you. Kind of pretty actually.

"Thank you," said Entity.

"So you are female?" Paul blurted out, surprised by his brashness.

"I am neither male nor female, at least not anymore," Entity stated.

"Really? Because you actually look a little like my wife," Paul said somewhat sarcastically, now totally flummoxed.

"A reflection of what you were thinking."

Paul twitched a little nervously. "I guess I better watch what I'm thinking about a little more closely."

"You don't need to worry. We simply presumed your wife's likeness would make you feel more comfortable."

"It's a little weird, but I understand the rationale. Besides, you look good, but not as good as the real thing." Entity smiled agreeably, and Paul continued. "So are you here, or is your body somewhere else, like mine is?"

"I have no body anymore. Not in the way you do."

"Well, I seem to be striking out on all counts here. I hope I haven't offended you?" Paul said, feeling somewhat embarrassed.

"There is no need to feel remorse," Entity told him. "My body died many thousands of your years ago. I now exist only in the form you see."

"And what form is that?"

"It is very hard to explain. We live on the boundary of matter and energy. We have learned how to transition between the two, like ice transitions to water or water to vapor."

"How do you do that? With computers, or machines?"

"Those things did play a part at one time. In the beginning we were much like you, but that history is so old as to be nearly unrecoverable for us now. Between technological advancements and with the need to relocate our civilization—

"Relocate? Why?" Paul asked, astounded by the sheer prospect of such an endeavor.

"Various reasons. A rogue asteroid in one instance. In another, the star in a solar system we relocated to eventually exhausted its fuel and turned into a red giant, which threatened to swallow our planet. These kinds of events happened many times over the millennia, and ultimately reaching back to our beginning was no longer possible. Only remnants of our mythological roots remained, but those roots spoke to the struggles that we had endured that have gotten us to where we are presently."

"But you say you died years ago? How can you be here today? *What* are you doing here?" Paul waited for an answer, totally mystified.

"While bodies may die, thoughts evolve and, harnessed with technology, can live on. In the distant past, those who made up our society lived in several different states of existence over the course of their lives. One was our natural state, the organic beings we were born into. Then as we aged and our bodies began to wear out, we replaced the broken parts with synthesized organs. When life could no longer be sustained with synthesized organs, which usually took many hundreds of years, we transferred a person's memory map to an encoded replica of the person's former body and mind."

"Like artificial intelligence, but with a specific person's thoughts and feelings," Paul offered.

"Precisely. Over many eons we merged with our technology, and those two components continued to evolve together, eventually learning how to manipulate the interface between matter and energy. At that point we had no more need of the replicas."

"So there are more of you?" asked Paul, a little afraid of the answer.

"Now spread out across much of this universe and a few others."

"Others?"

"Others," replied Entity.

"Do you communicate with these others?" Paul asked, highly skeptical about what he was hearing.

"Constantly. We have found various ways to employ something that your scientists refer to as quantum entanglement. Communication is one of them."

"My understanding of entanglement is pretty limited, but I know you can't communicate information that way."

"But we can and do," Entity assured him. "We have been doing so for eons."

"What you're implying is immortality," Paul said incredulously.

"No one or thing is immortal. But we do live long, happy, productive existences. And that is what we want the people of Earth to experience."

"What do you mean?" Paul asked, feeling like they might be getting to the crux of the conversation.

"We are here to facilitate your survival."

"How?" Paul asked, intrigued and simultaneously cautious.

"We have already begun a campaign to restrict your ability to wage violence on each other."

Paul thought about this for a moment and then felt a derisive smirk spreading across his face. "That's not going to work. It never has. Violence is in us. It's part of what makes us who we are."

"It was in us too. A long time ago," Entity said calmly.

"You don't understand."

"But we do, and now that we are here, we will change that."

"What are you going to do?"

"What we have done on many planets that were at the same crossroads as you."

"What crossroads are you referring to?"

"Everyone armed to the teeth. No one trusting each other. Technological advancement far outpacing emotional development."

"How did you come to that conclusion?" Paul asked sardonically.

"From electromagnetic broadcasts from Earth."

"You mean you watched television?"

"Yes. And listened to the radio. It's how we acquired your languages, listened to your news, saw your violent entertainments, and realized how troubled your planet was."

"I can't deny that," Paul laughed.

"We can't eliminate all violence, but we can remove many of the mechanisms for it: guns, missiles, bombs."

"You've got to be kidding. You can't do that." Paul felt his temper flair somewhat.

"But we can. We can monitor the thoughts of everyone on Earth. We know who is thinking of violence, and their thoughts tell us what they're going to do, when they're going to do it, and where all their weapons are. People are rarely able to hide their thoughts, and removing the means of executing the violence is what we attempt to do. After that is accomplished, you will be free to evolve and progress on your own."

"You couldn't possibly remove all weapons. Do you know how many guns are on the planet?"

"Yes."

"Seriously?" Paul was inclined to believe Entity was telling the truth.

The alien continued, "Besides, the majority of people are *nonviolent*. The ones who are *not* nonviolent stand out. At the point at which the violence falls to near zero, we will know we have accomplished our task."

"What you're proposing is impossible."

"Quite the contrary. We have done this many times before. Intelligent life in the cosmos is too extraordinarily precious to let it kill itself. If we allowed that to happen to you, now that we know you are here, we would feel responsible for your deaths, so we intercede on your behalf, like good parents protecting their children. But I assure you it is nothing to be afraid of. A world without violence is really quite achievable."

"There's no way you could do that. Take away all the weapons?"

"But I assure you we can. And after many generations have existed without the means to kill, beyond what is essential for survival, violence will quite naturally disappear. There are only a few civilizations out of thousands we have helped where that has not been so. But in almost every case, they all started out like you saying 'never.' And 'never' is what we must work to change."

"You're serious?" Paul said, still not believing what he was hearing.

"Absolutely."

"So how does all this work?" Paul asked, trying to get a grip on what he was going to tell those at Galaxy. "The building, the glass room, the fog, transporting me, the snatching of weapons—how does this all work?"

"It would be impossible to explain. But the short answer is that we think it and it happens."

"That's crazy. Think of something. A door?" Paul challenged.

Entity pointed to an outside wall that was previously entryway free. Paul quickly turned his head and noted a new curtain of light now splitting the wall in half.

"Okay, I concede it looks like you can do what you say, or think, that is. But there has to be a mechanism."

"There is," the alien admitted. "And hopefully your species will live long enough to discover it for yourselves. However, it's not something we can give you. It's something you must grow into, like adulthood."

"So you're saying we're children?" Paul quipped.

"In an evolutionary sense, yes. But children with the means to destroy one another. We would not want to add to that ability."

Paul could see that at this moment Entity was deadly earnest. He waited for further explanation, but none was forthcoming. "So that's it? You're going to do this no matter what?" he said, utterly disheartened, and still not sure he believed any of it.

"Yes. That's it," Entity assured him.

With that Paul woke up in his CQ. He could feel sweat on his forehead, and for the first time, he wished that what he had experienced had been a dream. Instead it was a nightmare. But a real nightmare, and he was sure the world was not going to go down without a fight. But as the day progressed, he began to ask himself why the idea seemed so frightening. If such a thing were possible and if the entity actually could bring about such a change, wouldn't it be a miracle?

The next day onboard the space station, Martina informed Paul that his EKG looked perfectly normal and that he had "slept like a baby." She also informed him that another videoconference had been scheduled for later in the day, this one with Galaxy Enterprises and a three-star general from the Department of

Defense. To Paul that was an ominous sign, but the timing gave him a good portion of the day to ruminate about how to approach things. He noted to himself that while he had been disturbed by what Entity had said on some deeply personal, fundamental level, he never felt any sense of impending doom. In actuality, the annoyance he felt was more akin to when he was a child and his parents would give him a time-out and send him to his room; only in this case it was a cosmic time-out.

In relaying the information during the afternoon videoconference, Paul did his best to stress the nonaggressive nature of what the entity was proposing, but it all fell on deaf ears. General Tillard, the DOD representative, expressed his desire for Paul to stay in contact with the alien, not to glean more information but for the vital purpose of keeping an eye on the entity. While the general personally believed the idea of confiscating everyone's weapons was totally preposterous, in the interest of national security, he would insist that NASA continue with their plan to send a probe to the moon. He also endorsed an accelerated program to get astronauts back on the moon to counter the threat.

"What threat?" Paul asked the general somewhat innocently.

"You're not serious, are you?" the general responded. "You can't take away someone's means of protection and say it isn't a threat."

"I thought you said the idea was preposterous? Besides, if they can do what they say they can do, what would be the problem?"

"The problem is they can't do it," the general responded abruptly.

"But we don't know that," Paul countered. "Based on what they've demonstrated so far, it might just be possible. I've been on the moon four times now. And I spoke with my wife on the moon."

"Or so you think," the general corrected.

"General, with all due respect, I am well past the point of believing that what I have experienced is happening only in my mind and that my wife is some kind of accessory to my delusions."

Ken Ishida sensed that Paul was getting a little hot under the collar and jumped into the conversation in an attempt to divert Paul before he got himself into hot water. "Paul, we have no hard evidence that what you *say* is happening is *actually* happening."

"What?" Paul said in disbelief.

Ken went on. "It's true there is something happening on the moon, but we cannot be certain that what you have experienced is real. If what you say is true, if these beings are really that advanced, they could be exerting some type of mind control, trying to get you to persuade us to do their bidding. To roll over and play dead. To do so could jeopardize our national security. We have to proceed with caution."

"Paul," said the general, softening a bit, "we take you at your word. But we have to approach this with some skepticism. Otherwise we could be playing into their hands. As I understand it, to the best of our knowledge, your body never left the space station. Is that right?"

"Affirmative, sir."

"Then we cannot be sure it is really happening, and a defensive posture is imperative under that circumstance. But stay in contact. Learn what you can. And keep us apprised."

"Yes, sir."

The videoconference ended, and Paul could not help but feel he had not handled things very well. It was hard for him to know which side he should be on: he understood both points of view.

The epidemic of gun thefts was accelerating around the world, so much so that there ensued a worldwide panic to purchase. At retail outlets, however, guns were inexplicably disappearing from shelves, leaving none for buyers to purchase. Gunmakers' assembly lines were cranking out weapons, but they seemed to disappear in transit to stores. Eventually equipment on some assembly lines stopped working.

Rumors that aliens were responsible for the robberies began to circulate on social media, but in the beginning no one was taking them seriously. But the rumors persisted and appeared to be originating in Houston. Paul could only watch from onboard the space station as it all unfolded, powerless to stop it, while secretly marveling that the aliens appeared to be making good on their promise. While he hoped the rumors were a product of leaks coming out of Galaxy or NASA's Johnson Space Center, it occurred to him that Rianne could also be the source.

"Did you tell anyone about your discovery, Ri?" Paul asked the girl during their next family videoconference.

"I didn't mean to, Dad. I was approached by a reporter outside my school."

"Outside your school?" said Paul, appalled by the apparent audacity of such a thing.

"She said she knew you were my father and also an astronaut and said she talked to someone at Galaxy who told her about aliens on the moon. Then she asked me if I knew anything, and I told her that I was the one who found them. I thought she was nice, and it wasn't until after she went away that I realized she might have tricked me. I don't know if she knew something or not."

"It's all right, Ri."

"I know, Dad. But I'm sorry. I know I wasn't supposed to say anything."

"It was bound to get out sometime, sweetheart. I wouldn't worry about it."

"Well, I'm worried about it," Lisa chimed in.

"How so? asked Paul.

"Because some of the kids have been harassing Rianne."

"Why would they do that?" Paul questioned Lisa, feeling totally helpless.

"Because they think she might be helping the aliens steal their family guns," Lisa said, dismayed over the absurdity of the accusations. "I am seriously thinking about going out and getting a firearm myself these days, except I don't know if I could find one now."

"I hate to hear you even say that, Lisa. It's not who you are," Paul said, trying to reason with her while admiring her motherly instincts.

"You'd be surprised by who I am when it comes to protecting my kids," she said with astounding sincerity.

"Rianne, are you feeling in danger at school?" Paul asked the girl with genuine concern.

"No, Dad. I have a lot of friends, and they hang with me. And the people who are mad know you're an astronaut, and they're afraid you might be friends with the aliens."

"Did you tell them that?" Paul asked with a bit of anger in his voice.

"No, Dad. I told them that's stupid. I told them you were on the space station, not the moon."

"Good girl," Paul said, feeling a bit like Judas. "Ri, do you think you could give your mother and me a few minutes by ourselves? There's something I need to talk to her about before I go."

"Is it about the moon?" his daughter asked, obviously worried she was not to be trusted anymore.

"I think you have a birthday coming up soon, don't you?" Paul asked in a tone that carried a kind of implied hazard.

"Yes."

"Well, if you want anything from me, I need some time with your mom. Alone!"

"Yes, sir." The girl immediately launched herself up and out of the chair, said "I love you, Dad," and departed at the speed of light.

"Well, that was a flash of inspiration," Lisa said, though still clearly agitated by the previous discussion.

"Are you really worried?" Paul asked Lisa as soon as their daughter was out of earshot.

"Do you know there was another school shooting today, Paul? And yesterday a bomb exploded on an elderly lady's front doorstep. And gas attacks on civilians overseas. And children being abducted and turned into sex slaves and soldiers. And McKenzie died this morning because a bullet struck her heart, and now my own son won't even talk to me and says he hates me!" Lisa, who was strong and normally composed, was now in tears.

"Lisa, I'm so sorry. But it's not your fault. Nick knows that. He's just hurting right now, so he lashes out."

"Well, I'm hurting right now too, and I *am* worried. I don't know what the world is coming to, and I am hoping that your aliens can do something about it. And I wish to God you were here."

"I'm sorry, Lisa."

"It's not your fault. I know that. It's just that the world is such a mess it's hard to be optimistic about the future."

"I know. But you're doing more than your share to help it. And I'm sure that McKenzie and her family knew how hard you were trying."

"I sure hope so, because I was." Lisa wiped her eyes and then looked back at the screen. "I'm sorry, Paul. I shouldn't have done that to you."

"You didn't do anything to me, Lisa. You're my wife, and you were honest with me. And I wish I was there to support you."

"You do support me, Paul. Always. Always."

"I love you, Lisa."

"I love you too, Paul." Lisa kissed her finger and then pressed it to the computer's webcam before ending the call.

Paul sat for a while staring ahead blankly and then said out loud, "Entity, I need to talk."

"Are you sure you aren't making things worse?" Paul asked Entity. "I worry that things could spiral out of control. You have no idea how outraged people in my country can be when it comes to having their guns taken away."

"We do know. Right now we are in the process of thinning the stockpile of new weapons, taking the most lethal ones first. We have taken very few weapons from private citizens yet, though we have confiscated some from people whose intentions seemed questionable."

"And people are panicking," Paul insisted.

"Yes. They're afraid, because they don't understand."

"I don't see how that can be good," Paul persisted.

"Fear is necessary to survival. But like everything else, it must be moderated, such as when people use weapons to strike fear into those around them. Therefore those weapons must be removed."

"But not everyone is trying to strike fear into others. Some just seek protection from that fear."

"It is rare to find an intelligent society that has emerged from its history without a propensity to kill. Typically it is encoded in their genetic material long before they even know what that is. But like the chrysalis transforming itself into a butterfly, at some point society must go through the difficult process of peaceful transformation if it is to survive and thrive. That is what we are here to foster: your next stage of evolution."

"That's a little arrogant, don't you think?" Paul said indignantly.

"But we're not looking down on you," said Entity. "If anything we have great admiration for you. Perhaps inoculating your society against a dreaded disease would be a better analogy."

"But it's like you're playing God. What right do you have to come here and preach to us about our evolution? You evolved. You lived. You were free to do it your own way. Make your own mistakes."

Entity remained silent for a long moment, studying Paul. Then Paul heard Entity's thoughts proceeding slowly and calmly in his brain. "Most intelligent species are social and territorial. Man seems no different."

"He's not," Paul admitted.

"These traits have allowed him to build the civilizations that you have today."

"Yes. It has. And there are problems, I grant you. But humankind is not irredeemable," Paul said defensively.

"Of course not. We never thought that, or we wouldn't have bothered."

"But what you're doing, it's not your choice to make."

"So you think we should stop what we're doing?"

That question stopped Paul cold. "I didn't say that exactly." Paul's expression was pained.

"But what you're inferring is that you have hope for humankind? You feel they can sort their problems out for themselves?"

Paul could feel himself being boxed in. He could also hear Lisa's voice in his head, expressing the hope that the aliens could fix things on Earth. "I don't know, but it seems like humans ought to be given the chance to try."

"Do you think we should leave?" the entity asked surprisingly matter-of-factly.

"What! Are you seriously asking me that?" Paul could hear himself almost shout.

"Why not? We've found no reason not to trust you."

Paul felt the weight of the question on his shoulders. Were the aliens truly prepared to give humans a choice? It was not a position he liked being in, but here it was. "And if I said yes, would you? Leave?" Paul said, testing.

"Yes."

"Why? Why me?" Paul screamed out. "Why would you entrust the future of the whole world to my judgment? It makes no sense."

"Because we know what is in your heart. You are a decent man and an honest reflection of your species. Who better to decide?"

"I'm not a decent man or an honest reflection. I'm a flawed individual with a checkered past."

"You were a man put in a terrible position in war," Entity said, as if his entire past were an open book that the alien had read.

"And I killed someone who should be alive today to save someone who was contemptible. But he was an American soldier," Paul spoke derisively, the pain of the experience still extremely raw.

"You killed because you had no choice under the circumstances you found yourself in."

"I'm not so sure."

"You're a good person, Paul."

"I'm the wrong person to make this decision."

"You are the perfect person," Entity said, trying to soothe him.

"No."

"Then name someone. A group of people who could decide if you prefer."

"A group! Heavens no! That would be worse."

"Then someone who you think would make a more responsible decision than you."

Paul laughed. "My wife."

"And what would she say?"

"I think she would tell you to stay. But I'm not absolutely sure. And she's not being asked to make the decision. I am. And I don't know what to say."

"Then we will give you time to sleep on it, as your people say."

Paul could tell from past conversations that Entity was about to transport him back to his CQ, but on some deep, instinctual level, he already knew what choice he wanted to make, even if people hated him for it.

"Can I ask a favor?" Paul asked in his search for an answer.

"You want to speak to your wife," Entity assumed.

"I'm surprised. Actually, I wanted to speak to my daughter, Rianne. I thought you were reading my mind?"

"We do our best to honor the privacy of people's thoughts whenever we can."

"Could you arrange that?" Paul asked. "Let me see her?"

"Why?"

"Clarity of thought, unencumbered by politics or money. Just simple, straightforward innocence. Could you arrange that?"

"Of course."

That evening Rianne kissed her mother good night and retired to her room. A short while later, as she lay in bed, stroking Ralph's furry head, her thoughts turned to her father on the space station. Slowly her mind relinquished the day, and she drifted off to sleep. Or so she thought.

Rianne woke in a room shrouded with fog. Her first thought was that she was having a nightmare, but it seemed far too real for that. Then she heard a familiar voice.

"Rianne."

Rianne took a few steps forward toward the sound of the voice, stopping only after clearing the fog. Not knowing what to think when she saw her father, she simply said, "Dad! Is that really you?"

"More or less, sweetheart."

"How did we get here? I thought you were on the space station."

"I am. And I'm here as well. Just like you."

"Where are we?" the girl asked, still unsure if any of this was real.

"We're on the moon, Ri."

"How can that be?" Rianne asked with great apprehension.

"I'll show you." Paul spoke those words, and the fog dissipated. And Rianne found herself in the glass-like, enclosed room, looking out at the lunar landscape.

"How did we get here?" she asked as she peered through the clear barrier.

"You remember the other day when you told the kids at school I was on the space station and didn't know the aliens?"

"Yes."

"Well, that wasn't true. In fact, I am the only person who's met them so far."

"For real?" Now the girl was excited.

"For real. But it's not as simple as that."

"How so?"

"Entity, the alien I communicate with, wants me to make a decision about something, and I don't know what to do. I need some advice."

"From me?"

"Yes."

"What kind of advice? You already know everything, Dad."

"I only wish that were true, Ri."

"It's true, Dad. You're the smartest person I know."

"Which is why I asked one of the smartest people I know to come here and talk to me."

"Me?" the girl said, pointing at her chest with pride.

"Yes, you."

"What do you want to talk about?"

"The aliens are here for a very specific reason, Ri. They've been studying us, and they think they can help us, but I'm not sure they can. I mean I'm sure they can do what they say, but I don't know if it will be good for us in the long run. I don't know if it will solve the problem or just make it worse?"

"Do you mean a problem for you and me and Nick and Mom?"

"I mean for the world. For all humankind, Ri."

"I don't understand."

"How did you feel when those kids were killed at the high school?"

"Terrible. I was angry. I felt like it shouldn't have happened."

"What would you have done to stop it?"

"I would have taken the gun away from the person who shot them, if I could have."

"What if someone could take away all the guns? From everywhere and everyone. How would that feel?"

"How could they do that? They say almost everybody has guns."

"I don't know how they could do it, but just suppose they could, even if we didn't understand how?"

"Gee, Dad, I don't know. I think a lot of people would be really mad. It would be stealing."

"In a sense that's true. But what if they could really do it anyway? Do you think they should? Do you think we should let them?"

"I don't know, Dad. I don't think you *could* take all the guns away, which means you would need guns because people would be fighting for their guns, so I think you'd have to get a gun to fight the aliens that were taking your guns." When she finished, her eyes were wide and innocent.

"I see. It's a vicious circle," Paul said as he tried to follow the young girl's logic.

"Yes, sir. It is."

"So you wouldn't want to live in a world without guns or violence or fear then?"

"Well, when you put it like that, it sounds nice. Like heaven. But I don't see how that could happen."

"It's what the aliens are proposing to offer us, and I brought up many of the same things you just mentioned. And they decided to leave the choice as to whether they go or stay up to me."

"Gee, Daddy, what are you going to tell them?"

"What would you tell them, Ri?"

"You think they're really smart?"

"Oh, yes. Even smarter than me, sweetheart. And very advanced. If I asked them to change this room into something else, they could do it." With that the room began to rematerialize into the cathedral-like structure.

"Wow! This is cool!" the girl said, looking around the open interior space as it continued forming around them.

"So what do you think you would say?" her father implored once the transformation was complete.

"I think I would have faith they could do it," she said, turning back to her father. "I don't hate guns, but I don't like them either. I hate when people are hurt by them though, and I think we'd probably be better off if they were all gone, or if at least bad people didn't have any."

If they do this, they want me to speak to the people of Earth and explain what's happening. A lot of people are going to be really furious at me and maybe you as a result."

"I can take it. I'm sure my friends will still like me."

"Let's hope so."

"Why are they doing this, Daddy?"

"To save us from ourselves, I think. They want to give us time to wash the instinct to kill out of our systems."

"You mean like our DNA, like we learned about in school?"

"Something like that," Paul smiled.

"I don't know what to tell you, Dad. But I think I would probably tell them to go ahead and see what happens. Just think of all the things we could learn from them."

With that simple statement, all the pieces fell into place for Paul, and he found himself alone with Entity once again.

"Rianne?" Paul questioned Entity.

"At home, in bed, asleep."

"I didn't get a chance to say goodbye. Will she remember?"

"Do you want her to?"

"If she's going to have to deal with the consequences, she might appreciate understanding what it's all about."

"I take it you've decided?" Entity said softly.

"You probably knew all along."

"No one knows anything with any certainty," the alien freely admitted. "It's a probabilistic universe."

"Quantum uncertainty."

"Yes. And brains are the most extreme expression of quantum uncertainty yet devised."

"Well, I'm certain of this: I want you to stay and keep doing what you're doing. I'm certain I would eventually regret it if I told you to leave. Even my daughter's initial answer was to get a gun. That can't be good."

"It is a conundrum. At some point guns must become an anachronism. Better sooner than later," the alien said simply.

"So what do you need from me?"

"We need you to be our ambassador, to speak to your people. In your position as an astronaut, you're the perfect spokesperson."

"I'm not so sure. And I worry about my family."

"We know. And we will do everything in our power to keep them safe."

Paul was silent, still wrestling with whether what he was doing was for the best, but committed to pursuing the goal. "I'm truly frightened," Paul acknowledged to Entity. It was the first time he felt that way since he first encountered the alien. "I've never made a decision for the whole world before."

"It takes courage," Entity said in a reassuring voice. "And you have just given your world a very healthy dose of it."

"Really?" said Paul. "Because at the moment, I'm not feeling so sure of it."

"Come on," said Entity. "Let me take you on a tour."

Lisa was worried about her daughter's inability to wake even with poking and prodding but soon suspected what the problem was. When the girl finally opened her eyes, she seemed somewhat disoriented.

"I saw Papa, Mom."

"I thought as much," Lisa told the girl.

"We were on the moon. But I don't know how I got there."

"I was there with your dad a few days ago too. But I don't know exactly how I got there either."

"He said the aliens wanted to get rid of all the guns and they were asking him if he thought they should do that. Or did he want them to leave? He was asking me for advice, but I didn't know what to say. Why is it such a hard question?"

"It just is, Ri," Lisa responded distantly, reality hitting her like a ton of bricks. At that moment Lisa realized the rumors were all true, and finally understood the full extent of Paul's dilemma.

"But why? Everyone hates when people get killed. And if nobody had any guns, then nobody would get killed."

"I'm sure people would find other ways to hurt each other."

"But there would probably be a lot less killing, wouldn't there?"

"Perhaps."

"Then shouldn't we let the aliens take the guns?"

"It's a matter of trust, Ri. A matter of trust and fear."

"I don't understand why it's so complicated."

"Because we're all human, and human beings are complicated, with complicated pasts."

"So what do you think Daddy will do?"

"His best. He will do his best to make the right decision."

"But what will that be?"

"I don't know, Ri. But I bet he's thinking about it really hard, right as we speak."

"We want you to keep talking to this Entity and see if you can find any cracks." Though General Tillard wished Paul was still in uniform and under his direct command, he suspected the now civilian astronaut was the only person the aliens would allow to act as a liaison between themselves and Earth.

"I haven't seen any weaknesses so far, General," Paul offered.

"Every enemy has weaknesses, son. You just need to find them."

Paul decided to ignore the general's patronizing comment. "Why do you consider them an enemy, sir?"

"Do I really need to say it? They want to remove our defenses. That's what enemies do."

"I don't think that's their intent, General."

"Then how would you describe it?"

"I think they want to help us eliminate violence. In fact, their goal is our survival."

"You're being naïve, Mr. Connors," the general reasoned. "They're inviting chaos. Think what you like about guns and bombs and missiles, but in reality they keep the peace, not to mention providing us with thousands of jobs."

"But at what cost, sir?"

"Better to live with fear than to die without it, don't you think, Paul?" Ken Ishida interjected.

"Whose side are you on, Ken?" Paul snapped, reprimanding his boss.

"Our side, Paul," Ken said. "The human side."

Paul was exasperated. "General, I don't think you understand. I believe this is going to happen whether we like it or not. I don't see any way for us to stop it."

The general pulled up close to the computer screen and spoke to Paul in a whisper. "We have a mission in the planning stages as we speak. Without being specific, it is a mission that will shed a lot of light on the subject and solve our problem once and for all."

"What are you proposing?" asked Paul out loud.

"Let's just say," whispered the general, "that we can make life extremely toxic for them on our moon."

"You know, whispering is not going to help," Paul said rather belligerently. "They're probably reading our thoughts as we speak. They are light years ahead of us, General."

"All the more reason to force them to leave as quickly as possible," the general insisted in a normal tone of voice.

"There's no need to force them," Paul blurted out. "They already offered to leave on their own." He knew he'd stepped in it now.

"Then why haven't they?" Ken asked suspiciously.

"Because I couldn't bring myself to tell them they should," Paul answered.

"Are you saying they left the decision up to you?" the general demanded to know.

"They asked what I thought, and I told them," Paul responded.

"Why would you tell them to stay, Paul?" Ken asked in bewilderment. "Why would you make a decision like that on your own without even consulting any of us?"

"I wasn't exactly in a position to get back to you in that moment. Besides, I already knew what your response would be. They already knew it too. And the fact is they are probably our one and only best chance."

"At what?" the general asked cynically.

"At survival." Judging by the looks of the two men, Paul knew he had said way too much.

"You have a lovely family, Paul," the general said in a tone that hinted at a veiled threat. "I would hate to see anything happen to them if this thing should go south, if you catch my drift."

"Are you threatening my family, General?" Paul said, his eyes glaring.

"No. I'm saying they will be exposed to the anger of everyone who sees you as a traitor to their cause."

"And what cause would that be, General?"

"Their right to defend their lives and families, pure and simple. A little thing called the Second Amendment."

"Paul, you're our best hope here," Ken said, hoping to draw down the conversation's temperature a bit. "We need your cooperation. Your family needs your cooperation. Their survival may depend on it."

"Isn't anyone interested in negotiating with this life form? Isn't anyone in the least bit interested in what they have to offer us before you jump into a fight with them?"

"We don't see that we have much time to negotiate," the general shot back. "That train has already left the station. You were right about what they were planning. Guns are jumping off store shelves, but not into the hands of buyers. They're just disappearing. They're disappearing from private citizens' homes and starting to disappear from the military as well. Now I don't know how that is happening, but I know that the situation is getting dangerous. People don't know what is going on, or why? And those who still have guns are thinking they need to use them. And we need to take immediate action to stop that from happening."

"Then let me address the nation, and the world, from the space station. Reassure people that the aliens mean them no harm."

"No!" The general's patience had reached its limit. "You really don't know that they mean us no harm. It's total speculation."

"I'd trust my family's safety to them," Paul said confidently.

"Then you're a bigger fool then I thought," the general responded.

"I've met them and talked to them, General."

"You met one of them, and that's all. And for all you know, your Entity might not even be real. Maybe nothing more than a sophisticated computer generation."

"Or maybe Entity is an angel in disguise," Paul suggested with a touch of cynicism.

"Look, Connors," the general said, seething, "let me make myself perfectly clear. You either help get the aliens to leave and set things right, as they were before they got here, or you try and get us enough technical information to destroy them. Those are your choices, and if you want to see your family again, you better make the right one."

"General . . ."

"And there won't be any more calls home until we are out of this mess. Is that understood? Ken?"

"Yes, General," Ken responded sheepishly.

"I want him cut off from Earth completely except for you," the general said, pointing directly at Paul's image on his computer.

"You won't stop them," Paul said, this time keeping his cool.

"We'll see about that." The general disappeared from Paul's screen.

"Won't you reconsider, Paul? For your family's sake? For the company's sake? If you don't help, Galaxy might never get another government contract."

"If I give in, humankind may never get another chance like this again. It's not about money for these aliens. Don't you understand? They don't want to destroy us; they want us to live and prosper. Put a price tag on that."

"Think on it, Paul. I will speak with you tomorrow." With that Ken disappeared from Paul's screen as well.

Paul returned to his CQ, wondering how he was going to survive without being able to communicate with his family. The general viewed himself as a man of his word and would see to it that Paul was indeed cut off. Yet in the back of Paul's mind, he was certain that the general's ability to counter the alien plan was woefully inadequate. Paul had no doubts that the aliens could do what they intended; he had seen their powers up close. But perhaps Ken and the general were right in that Paul really hadn't had sufficient contact with the aliens to accurately judge their character. If Paul was wrong, it could spell disaster for the entire planet. But his mind kept going back to the peace he and

Lisa had felt in the alien presence. Was that real or simply some psychological trick?

Paul came out of his CQ just as Martina was coming back from working in the lab. She brought a couple of lab-grown grape tomatoes, offering Paul one upon seeing him.

"Thanks." Paul popped the tomato in his mouth and bit down. "Wow! Now that's delicious," Paul said as he did his best to contain the juice in his mouth.

"I thought you would like it. Space grown, organic, and fresh!"

"It's terrific." Paul noticed Martina eyeing him closely but decided to ignore it. "How'd it go today?" he asked her instead.

"Good. I got nearly everything done that was scheduled. How are you?" she asked somewhat guardedly.

"Why do ask?" Paul said, equally cautious.

"Because I was told to limit my interactions with you. I figured something must be up."

"The general?" Paul asked.

"Actually, it was Ken who gave me the word, but I sense it was the general pulling the strings."

"Yes. He's quite the diplomat." Paul studied Martina's face, unsure of what she knew, but certain he needed someone to confide in. "Do you know what's been happening to me, Martina?"

"Some."

"Some?"

"Word has it that you have been in contact with an alien on the moon. Reports from Earth indicate that personal firearms are disappearing at an alarming rate. No one knows how, but word has leaked to the general public that aliens are on the moon, and panic is building. And the general is angry because you won't do anything about it. That's what I know in a nutshell."

Paul affirmed her information with a nod of his head. "That pretty much sums it up. But what they didn't tell you is how advanced these aliens appear to be. Or how much they want to help us."

"Are you sure of that?" Martina asked Paul.

"Are you spying for the general or for Ken maybe?" Paul asked.

"I'm spying for myself and my husband and children. Because if I had a wish, it would be for a world free of guns, and I think if there is any way you could help make that happen, I would kiss you for it."

"It's a tempting offer," said Paul. "But don't tell my wife."

"It will be our secret," the Italian said with a smile.

While Ken Ishida had no love for General Tillard, he shared some of the general's apprehensions about what was happening on the moon. In addition, he understood that while Galaxy was a private consortium, much of the organization's bread and butter was still tied to the US DOD.

Ken also harbored some concerns about Paul's state of mind. While he had always trusted Paul implicitly, he was also aware that Paul could have experienced some mind alteration to make him believe that the aliens were benign. As such Ken brought Dr. Price into his office to discuss the issue, but with no way to perform any advanced diagnostics, like an fMRI, there was no way to confirm anything one way or the other. In the end Ken found himself back at square one.

A few days later, there was another mass shooting, this one at an outdoor amateur sporting event. Two shooters drove onto the center of a football field, spraying the crowd with weapons fire, killing several spectators before police were able to shoot them. Gun-rights advocates claimed that had the fans been "packing heat," those attackers would have been dead as soon as they exited their vehicle.

Ken Ishida and a few members of the mission team were now the only people with whom Paul had contact. He was grateful that Ken used videoconferencing for the most part as it felt somewhat personal. And while Ken tried to follow the general's mandate of limiting Paul's earthly contacts, Ken was enough of a soft touch to keep Paul informed about his family's well-being. It was also possible that Ken knew that the aliens were fully capable of arranging meetings between Paul and his family against the general's wishes, and without the general's knowledge. This was a good thing as far as Ken was concerned because he worried that depression could make Paul useless to the mission if the general put too much pressure on the astronaut. Paul's mission was scheduled for eighteen months minimum, and Ken doubted that the aliens would allow Paul to be brought down from the space station early. It was clear they had chosen Paul for a reason, and they weren't going to let him go, general or no general. The one thing Ken believed was that the aliens were as advanced as Paul was conveying.

"How are you feeling, Paul?" Ken asked the astronaut a couple of days after the general had announced his edict.

"I'm fine, Ken," Paul responded.

"I talked with Lisa this morning and told her about the general's order. She wasn't surprised because she had tried to call you but couldn't get through, but she wasn't worried either. She asked me to say hello to you, if that was still allowed."

"Is it?" Paul asked, with a wry smile.

"I think I can get away with it," said Ken, smiling back. "This is a real mess, Paul," Ken continued. "I feel uneasy about it, and I don't know how to resolve it."

"There may be nothing anyone can do to 'resolve it.' I think that's Entity's point."

"What do you mean?"

"We need to accept what's happening, not resolve it."

"That would take a lot of faith, Paul, in something we don't understand."

"True. But then, we're not being left with much choice."

"But you said they asked you if they should stay or go."

"And I came close to telling them to go. But I couldn't. My own daughter convinced me that would be a mistake."

"How so?" Ken inquired.

"By explaining to me, in a very roundabout way, that we probably have to fight the aliens, or we'll end up fighting each other."

"And she's likely right. Which would mean it would be best for the aliens to leave, don't you think?"

"It's like an endless loop," Paul said, quiet and despondent. "It always has been. That the only way to deal with violence is with violence. I don't want to condemn my son or daughter to that."

"Paul, Rianne is being practical. You should take a lesson from her."

"Rianne has never been given a choice. We are killers at heart, and we have a chance to change that."

"Paul . . ."

"Five- and six-year-old children and their teachers were shot at their school, and we couldn't even manage a reasonable conversation about doing away with assault weapons. That conversation was totally off the table. What the hell is that about?"

"Paul, you need to ask Entity to leave now," Ken said softly, hoping for a simple resolution.

"I couldn't do that."

"Why?" Ken asked with nearly a whimper. "Surely they would allow you to change your mind?"

"I am sure they would. It's me who doesn't want to change theirs."

"People need to survive, Paul. They have a right to protect themselves. Self-preservation is not a crime."

"Of course not, but it's all gotten out of hand," Paul answered with a shake of his head. "Entity's plan is to remove all the weapons for a period of time . . ."

"How long?"

"As long as necessary. Until the instinct to kill, itself, dies."

"That will never happen, Paul. It's a fairy tale," Ken predicted.

"It has to happen. We don't think it's possible because we've never been given the opportunity to overcome our past, but this alien race can give us that. They've done it for others."

"Paul, you have no proof of that."

"I have all the proof I need, and I won't try to stop them."

"Did you ever think you may be dooming the world, Paul? Doesn't that scare you?"

"What scares me is passing up an opportunity to save it."

Ken waited a moment and then said with gravity, "The Department of Defense and NASA are planning an attack on the moon."

"When?" Paul wasn't surprised. He knew that the general had alluded to such a possibility.

"That's classified. There are some technical issues to work out, but the plan is solid and moving forward. I think it will happen very soon."

"I don't understand why we wouldn't be chomping at the bit to know more about these aliens, Ken?"

"I *am* chomping at the bit, Paul. But I also worry about my kids and the earth's future." Some anger was creeping into Ken's normally reasonable voice. "If your aliens are on the up-and-up, why don't they come down to Earth and speak with us directly? Why don't they give us some of their technology? If they are so omnipotent, why are they hiding on the moon, out of sight?"

"Because we're ready to bomb the hell out of them because they want to make the world a more peaceful place. They know that, Ken. They knew that would be our default position from the start, but they're not going to give us that opportunity."

"We seem to be at an impasse here," Ken said dejectedly.

"Let me talk to the press from the station," Paul implored.

"Now that would go over big with the general, wouldn't it?"

"He might not be happy, but it might put some of the public at ease," Paul said, trying to be reassuring.

"What we need to do is put *all* the public at ease," Ken countered.

"So what you're suggesting we do, Ken, is keep the status quo? Live with our guns forever?"

Ken shook his head and sat silently for a few seconds. "I'll have to think on it."

Paul's screen went blank. He couldn't help wonder what the next move would be.

The next morning Ken Ishida's wife tried desperately to wake him for work. While she could tell that he wasn't dead, she was certain he was having a heart attack or stroke. She dialed 911 and waited.

In the emergency room, doctors performed a series of tests but found nothing that could explain what was wrong. Ken's blood pressure was normal, and his heart was functioning perfectly: all his vitals looked good. However, they could not wake him, and under the circumstances they had no choice but to keep him under close observation.

It was early evening when Ken finally awoke, surprised to find himself in the hospital with his wife, Margaret, at his side. She was holding his hand through the rail of the bed and was pleased to see a smile appear on Ken's face as soon as his eyes opened.

"It's so good to see you smiling," Margaret said as she rose and kissed his forehead.

"Why am I here?" Ken inquired.

"I couldn't wake you this morning. I thought you may have had a heart attack or stroke."

Ken thought about telling Margaret the truth, but he decided to keep his visit to the moon a secret for the time being.

"How are you feeling?" Margaret asked her husband.

"Never better," was his reply.

The aliens' initial appearance on the moon had been so low key that the little information that dribbled out wasn't given much consideration at first. But by the time the evidence mounted, a worldwide panic ensued. Overactive imaginations were part of the story, but most of the panic derived from anger engendered by the disappearance of people's personal arsenals. However, there was also a portion of the population that held out hope that there may have been some truth to the rumors that the aliens' intent was to confiscate all weapons.

The disappearance of weapons was accelerating, and there seemed to be a method of prioritization. Weapons at gun shows disappeared, even when guards were posted. If eyes were taken from a gun, even for a few moments or the blink of an eye, it was likely to be gone. If a weapon was purchased at a gun show, it was likely to disappear on the drive home or at the home itself. It was impossible to keep tabs on weapons every moment of every day, and a moment was all it took for them to disappear.

Militaries of authoritarian governments were targeted before more stable, democratic countries. And terrorist groups were also being stripped of guns and bombs. But it wasn't as though the terrorists were suddenly exposed and in fear for their lives. People who thought to take advantage of those whose weapons had disappeared, also found themselves without weapons. It was like the thoughts of the entire world population were under some cosmic microscope. Even law enforcement was subject to some scrutiny. Police with honest intent found their side arms still at their sides, while others found themselves without protection. One thing was becoming clear; little by little, all weapons were disappearing, except for what was absolutely essential.

World governments and organizations were in a quandary as to how to respond to the alien "menace," as it was called. Talks were held by the UN, NATO, the European Union, and other world organizations, but consensus was hard to come by.

Individual countries were trying to come up with their own solutions, but ultimately it was going to be up to the major powers to do something, and in all likelihood, the United States would shoulder most of the burden. The United States was in the best position to respond financially and technically, and since the country owned the preponderance of personal firearms, it was the most deeply affected. But not exclusively.

The president's cabinet had held a meeting with the Joint Chiefs, NASA scientists, and the CEO of Galaxy, during which General Tillard briefed the group on what Paul had conveyed to the general about his encounters with the entity. By this time there was little doubt that the information was accurate and that the aliens were proceeding with their plan. As a consequence, the conversation turned into a discussion of options: What measures could be taken to thwart the alien attempts? No one had a clue as to how the aliens were doing what they were doing, but it was assumed that there had to be an answer. The scientists present at the meeting talked about quantum mechanics, entanglement, relativistic travel, and a host of other topics, but it was all theoretical conjecture with nothing concrete. While the scientists may have been right about the amount of information they might be able to glean from an advanced race, the majority of those sitting around the table did not feel it worth the risk. The stakes were simply too high, with Earth's future in the balance. In a fit of frustration, the president's Chief of Staff recommended that Paul's family be held under house arrest or quarantined, whatever worked, so that they might force the astronaut to work with them against the "invaders." That option wasn't theoretical; it could be done immediately, and with impact. The astronaut claimed he had sway over the aliens, so let him prove it *and* prove his allegiance to the human race.

But there was resistance to that plan by those who suggested that it might be possible to negotiate terms with the aliens. But with the speed at which the aliens were achieving their goals, that idea seemed out of the question. At the rate things were going, negotiations would be a moot point within weeks, maybe days. Besides, the general had already made some decisions on his own.

In the end it was determined that the launch of a rocket with multiple thermonuclear warheads was their best option. Two of the scientists from NASA who sat at the meeting informed the group that should the president support the plan, that launch could happen within days. A heavy-lift rocket from Galaxy Enterprises was already in place and could be outfitted with multiple warheads with enough yield to cover much of the far side of the moon. The scientists guaranteed the president that this would solve his problem.

Rianne peeked through the drawn curtains as she and her mother were preparing to leave the house for school and work. It felt like a sea of people out front, some with signs protesting what was happening, a few signs heralding events, and what seemed like a battalion of police, soldiers, and reporters with cameras, trying to keep the peace or get information.

"Ri, Nick, are you ready?" Lisa was waiting at the door to the garage with purse in hand, and Rianne's backpack slung over her shoulder.

"I'll be there in a minute, Mom. I can't find my backpack," the girl shouted from her bedroom.

"I've got it with me, Ri," Lisa yelled back, a little peeved since she was running late. "I'll be in the car, you two."

"I'm staying home," was all she heard Nick say from somewhere in the house.

"Have it your way," Lisa muttered under her breath.

As soon as Rianne buckled in, Lisa pressed the garage door opener and waited for the door to rise. When it stopped she looked into the rearview mirror and was surprised to see two uniformed soldiers approaching the car, one on each side.

"Can I help you?" she said, lowering her window only part way.

"I'm sorry, Dr. Franklin, but we have orders to protect you and your children."

"So are you going to escort us to school and work?" asked Lisa, at first thinking this was pretty great.

"No, ma'am. Our orders are to keep you here at home," the young sergeant said as he cased the back seat of Lisa's vehicle.

"That's out of the question," Lisa responded rather vehemently. "I have patients to take care of at the hospital."

"The hospital's been alerted, ma'am. It's for your own protection."

"Protection from what? And on whose authority?"

"My understanding is that the White House authorized this last night. Sorry, ma'am."

"But we still need to get out, to get food and other necessities."

"Just give us a list, and we'll get it for you, ma'am," the young sergeant said politely.

"For how long?"

"For as long as we're told," he added.

The soldiers went back outside and stood in front of the garage door, which Lisa closed behind them.

"Do you believe this?" Lisa said, turning to her daughter.

"Why would they do this, Mom?"

"I think we both know the answer to that, Ri." Lisa and the kids weren't officially prisoners, but it sure felt like it.

Ken Ishida had not attended the White House meeting. As mission commander for this current space-station mission, such a thing was not possible, nor was he invited. However, the CEO of Galaxy Enterprises who had attended the meeting informed his employees upon his return of the "Go" decision made at the White House. But many of the company's staff scientists, engineers, doctors, and technicians had mixed reactions. On the one hand, a Galaxy rocket would play a pivotal role in the moon mission, but on the other hand, it was hard to estimate the amount of knowledge that would be lost in such a venture. While Galaxy technicians would certainly learn something from the launch, there was no doubt that the amount of information they would glean from the proposed mission would pale in comparison to the amount of information they might have picked up from such an advanced alien civilization. In that regard the sense of disappointment was profound.

Ken found himself even more conflicted. While he had no memory of meeting Entity the night he was taken to the hospital, he remembered in detail being on the moon. He remembered waking up in a fog-enshrouded, enclosed room on the moon, which then transformed into a kind of large cathedral-like structure. He was totally alone and explored the space on his own. At one point he found an entryway of light to what appeared to be the outside, and he went through, not really sure what would happen, and found himself in a secure environment, a kind of bubble encapsulating not only the building he had been in but also other structures. It was all quite beautiful, elegant, and peaceful. Though he met no one while he was there, it was clearly real, and he felt absolutely no sense of fear, knowing all the while he was safe. His perception of time however was totally distorted, because what felt like an hour on the moon nearly turned into a full day when he awoke in the hospital, which was ironic, because he had never felt better in his life.

"I'm going to try and arrange an interview for you," Ken told Paul on a secure channel, once he was released from the hospital.

"How did you get the general to approve?"

"He hasn't. I'm doing it on my own initiative," Ken stated.

"Why the change of heart?" Paul inquired.

"Let's just say I had a dream."

"Entity?"

"No. Something tells me you're the only one Entity is talking to. But I got a tour of sorts."

"And?"

"You know, they say a picture is worth a thousand words, but so is a feeling."

"Yes," Paul said with a rising inflection, trying to coax a more complete explanation from Ken.

"I think you're right," Ken continued. "I think it would be foolish to let them leave. I want to do what I can to help."

"What can I do?" Paul asked, buoyed by his colleague's change of heart.

"Nothing, for now. I'll handle it on this end. And I won't discuss it anymore until I have something lined up. The less said, the better. But I'm sure it won't be hard to get some reporter to talk to you."

"I suppose not," said Paul, smiling.

"Paul, there's one other thing. Your family is under a kind of house arrest right now," Ken said with a touch of remorse.

"I'm aware of that, Ken. But I trust that Entity will look after them."

"I'm sorry for not believing you."

"No worries. I didn't believe me myself for the longest time. It's all been a little weird."

"I'll be in touch," Ken said, and with that the channel closed.

The launch of the rocket was a highly anticipated event. A lot of people were afraid of the aliens, while others had come to the conclusion that they posed no immediate threat. Their biggest objection was that the aliens had no right to take away peoples' personal property. In general, the public gave little thought as to the treasure trove of information that was being tossed aside by the decision to obliterate the aliens.

The morning of the launch had a carnival-like atmosphere, quite similar to launches that took men and women into space. Normally missiles carrying bombs would have elicited negative reactions from all sorts of groups, but this was different. It was aliens feeling humankind's wrath for something they had done that was unjust, and with it came a sense of power for the people of Earth. These aliens were going to get their come-up-ins! Their due! The other thing was that the explosions were going to happen on the moon, and since there wasn't anything there anyway, it was expected to be quite a spectacular show, with little consequence for the earth. Kind of like a super New Year's Eve celebration. However, for safety reasons, spectators were kept at a much greater distance than normal from the launch site since the rocket carried a nuclear payload.

It was midmorning by the time the rocket was fueled, the weather cleared, and the countdown resumed. At T-minus ten seconds, the crowd started to hold its collective breath. At T-minus five seconds, almost everyone's hands went to their foreheads to block the glare of the sun, and at T-plus five seconds, everyone realized that something was wrong. The rocket just sat inert on the pad.

The crew at mission control scratched their heads, trying to figure out the cause of the failure to launch. Nothing on their computer screens gave any indication of what went wrong. But Ken Ishida knew what had happened, and rather than feeling frightened, he felt in awe of the aliens' technical ability to control events. To a devout Southern Baptist like himself, it was almost starting to feel like a second coming of sorts.

News of the failed attempt filled all the major media outlets, and the heads of state from the world's leading powers were holding emergency meetings with their cabinets and military leaders. The failure was a real shock to the world system, but even more profound shocks were to follow. World powers found their nuclear-delivery systems had been compromised and were now inoperative, but fearful of the potential imbalance of power this created, fought to keep the matter to themselves, often to no avail. Most countries were unsure as to whether it was the aliens who were responsible for shutting down their systems or whether some country on Earth was taking advantage of a situation and hacking into systems to cause more havoc.

The failed launch had a profound effect on the world. No longer did people feel safe or in control. Their moods darkened as a kind of malaise set in, and people distanced themselves from those they didn't know and even those they did.

Paul was dismayed by the news he was getting from Earth. He had always felt such tranquility when he was on the moon, but all he was seeing on Earth was mass anxiety. It was such an opposite effect from what he had envisioned that he once again began to wonder if he had made a colossal mistake in encouraging the aliens to stay. That night Paul found himself back on the moon.

"You're feeling like we've let you down," Entity said after emerging from the fog.

"Let's just say I was hoping it would all be a lot easier."

"We have found it is rarely an easy transition. There are many variables, and by the time we become aware of a civilization as advanced as yours, violence at many levels is usually woven into the social fabric. The struggle for survival naturally generates fear and anger."

"Isn't there anything you can do to help people adjust?"

"We tried many strategies but ultimately found removing the weapons of violence to be the most effective means of facilitating peace. And adjustment only comes with time."

"That's kind of funny."

"In what way?"

"When I was a kid, I watched a lot of science-fiction movies about space travel. It's what motivated me to become an astronaut. One had what they called a 'Prime Directive.'"

"*Star Trek,*" the alien said without hesitation. "Noninterference."

"You know of it?" Paul said with surprise.

"Yes. It is a principle we adhere to as well."

"But you *are* interfering, aren't you?"

"Only in one key aspect, without which there is little hope. We give civilizations an opportunity to live without violence long enough to make an objective choice."

"About what?"

"Whether they want to live a life dominated by fear and anger or one of relative peace and accord."

"Is that what I feel when I'm here, with you?"

"What you feel is the essence of my kind; who we have finally become, and what we have to offer you."

"What you have to offer seems almost too good to be true. Why hide out of sight on the moon?"

"We limit contact because fear and anger are contagious, in both good and bad ways. It's what your species refers to as the fight-or-flight response. It's protected you for thousands of years, but with technological advances it has outlived its usefulness and now poses a threat. And we know from what of our own past we can remember that we are not immune. Like doctors treating a deadly disease, we must protect ourselves. For us, the less contact we make, the better."

"So you're afraid of us?"

"We avoid any possibility of contamination. What we seek to do is create a situation where people are free to express themselves in every conceivable way, except through violence. We have been successful doing this in all but a few cases, but it always takes time. How much depends on the disposition of the society: At what level is their tendency for violence, which is always correlated to the amount of fear and anger present, both of which are always difficult to overcome."

"There must be something a race like yours, with all your technological sophistication, can do? The people on Earth feel exposed, and they're frightened."

"You can help that."

"I can't take away their fear. Or their anger."

"No. But you can show them *you* have no fear or anger."

"But I do have fear, and I do have anger. I had it for years after I got back from the war."

"But you redirected it. You put down your gun. You became an astronaut. You married and had children. You changed, and change is always difficult. Even change for the better."

"I'm not convinced this is right. I feel like I've made a terrible mistake."

"By asking us to stay?"

"Yes."

"Are you changing your mind? Do you want us to leave?"

"Yes. I think so."

Suddenly Paul was back in his CQ experiencing what appeared to be a lucid dream. In it all was quiet, but he didn't feel the peace he normally experienced after his encounters with the alien. He turned on his computer and tuned into a news broadcast, and there was not one word about aliens, guns disappearing, or failed moon launches. But there were reports of shootings, bombings, stabbings, and war, and Paul suddenly felt an overwhelming sense of loss. He looked up at the ceiling of his CQ with a pained expression on his face and whispered, "Entity? Are you still there?" At first there was nothing. Then Paul found himself back on the moon.

"You've made your point," he told the alien, feeling like he was caught in some galactic trap. "I don't want that either."

"The choice will always be yours. We will go if you ask. But you have to understand the consequence of that."

"Why? Why do you put so much trust in me?" Paul cried out in childlike bewilderment.

"Because you're good, but not perfect. And you are aware of it. We trust that quality in you. It makes you a reliable sounding board."

"But how can you be sure I'll make the right decision?"

"We're not. No one can be sure of anything. You know that. But in a quantum universe, we think there is a high probability that you will make the best choice for your people. We have faith in you. You have a good soul."

"Do you have a soul?"

Entity smiled. "You must judge that for yourself."

With that Paul was back on the space station.

The troops that were guarding Lisa and the kids were keeping a constant vigil on their home for several days now. Nick stayed in his room for the most part, angry with his mom for letting McKenzie die, angry with his dad for his part in the disappearance of weapons, and the continued alien presence, and particularly angry with his dad's attitude toward guns. Nick's request for a rifle on his birthday or for Christmas always fell on deaf ears. If he argued about it, his mom would give him a look that was meant to silence him and spare his father's feelings. Nick loved and admired his father, but he also resented having his life choices being dictated by his dad's experiences in war. Now he felt more adamant than ever. He had seen his friends killed and injured by a shooter, and he saw no reason why he shouldn't be given the chance to protect himself and the people he cared about.

On the other hand, Nick's sister and her dog were getting antsy. Their only recreational outlet was the backyard. It was relatively large and fenced in, but compared to the whole neighborhood in which Rianne normally roamed, it was fairly limiting. Still, Rianne was happy to get outside whenever she could, and the dog loved playing with her.

The backyard was surrounded by a slatted wood fence that had seen better days, and as luck would have it, Ralph found a slat that was unattached at the bottom. Before she knew it, Rianne saw the dog poking his nose through, moving the slat to the side, and slipping through the fence and disappearing. Panicked, Rianne worried that she might lose the dog if she didn't do something right away and quickly crawled through the opening after him. None of those guarding the house noticed.

For a change Paul was having a reasonably normal day all things considered. He was working in the lab on various experiments and enjoying Martina's company before she left the space station in a very few days. They were working with mice and enjoying their antics and the assorted ways the animals had adapted to being weightless. Paul knew that eventually he would be dissecting them as part of the overall experiment and was secretly wishing that Martina would be there to help, but he knew that would not be the case. A decorated combat veteran, Paul had become squeamish about killing anything for any reason, even in the interest of science.

About halfway through the day, Paul and Martina took a break and went back to their living quarters in Node 2 to have a bite to eat. As they were doing so, Paul's cell phone came to life.

"Paul, I have found someone relating to the matter we discussed previously." Ken's voice was soft, as though he were afraid someone was listening.

"Go on," Paul said, anticipating further details.

"We are working out the specifics and will get back to you within the next day or two. I just wanted to give you a heads-up so you can prepare."

"Thanks," Paul said, but it was doubtful Ken heard him as he quickly ended the call.

"That was cryptic. What was that about?" Martina asked Paul as she snacked on her last bite of food.

"You heard that?"

"Faintly," she said, swallowing.

"It was just something Ken asked me about a few days ago. He's got some scientist who wants to ask me a few questions about the aliens." Paul was hoping this simple lie would suffice.

"Just a few?" Martina joked. "I've got a thousand just to start."

"Like what?" Paul asked her with interest.

"Duh! Like where do they come from?" Martina said, laughing at her own basic question.

"I don't know that they're from anywhere anymore. At least not specifically. As near as I can tell, they are dispersed throughout space-time."

"How can that be? How can you not be from anywhere?" Martina said with a shake of her head.

"That I can't tell you. But I do know from the time I have spent with Entity that I am being shown an incredible amount but nowhere near what they could show me if they wanted to. I can't even fathom who these people, or whatever they are, are. Nor do I even begin to comprehend what they are capable of doing."

"That doesn't frighten you?"

"No. That's the only thing I know for sure. They're good, and I can't base that on anything except what I feel when I am with Entity."

"What's she like? Or he? Or whatever?"

"Like a gentle breeze. Always calm and reassuring. There and not there."

"Do you think they can really do what they say they will?"

"I have no reason to doubt them."

"But how is it possible?"

"I don't know, Martina. What was it Arthur C. Clarke once said? 'Any sufficiently advanced technology is indistinguishable from magic.'"

"That almost makes me feel like the mice in the lab," Martina said with a bit of discomfort in the comparison.

"That's just it; all I feel from them is compassion, and a sincere desire to see us survive, and thrive, with no strings attached."

"Total altruism? Come on, there are almost always selfish reasons for unselfishness."

"Perhaps, but I don't think in this case that holds true," Paul assured her. "I have a feeling that when they finish, they will leave. And that will be a sad day indeed, because once again we will be in a position to screw things up for ourselves."

"But you said you thought they would succeed. Doesn't that mean we would be changed?"

"Yes. And if they can do that, then it will surely be magic."

Lisa was beside herself. She was totally unaware of the break in the fence, which covered itself after the girl went through, swinging pendulum-like back into place from the single nail that was holding it up. She questioned Nick, who had no idea where his sister was, and the pair then searched throughout the house for Rianne, but she was nowhere to be found. It crossed Lisa's mind that Rianne might have tried to go to school, but it was so unlike Ri to do something like that and not say a word about it. Besides, how would she have snuck past the soldiers guarding the house?

Lisa and Nick went outside and spoke to a young female lieutenant who appeared to be in charge of watching them. When told of the girl's disappearance, the lieutenant seemed to suspect Lisa of trying to pull a fast one at first. But just to make sure, she gave Lisa the benefit of the doubt and went and searched the house herself. Finding no sign of the girl inside, she quickly called her commanding officer, who then referred the matter to General Tillard for instructions.

The general was not happy to hear of Rianne's disappearance and chastised the lieutenant for the escape. Convinced the girl could not go far and was still near her home, he ordered the soldiers to search the area and get her back, adding, "Heads will roll, if you don't."

As the lieutenant assembled the search detail, Lisa grabbed her arm, "Please, let me go with you."

"I can't do that, ma'am. I'm in enough hot water as it is."

"But I know the places she might be, and she's much more likely to listen to me than to trust you."

"If you have any ideas as to her whereabouts, just tell us, and we'll check them out. You'll just have to trust us on this."

"Please," Lisa implored."

"I'm sorry, Doctor."

"Then let my son, Nick, go with you. Please. She'll listen to her brother if you find her."

The lieutenant thought for a moment, and then, being a mother herself, she gave in. "All right." She looked at Nick and said, "Come with me. But no funny stuff, understand?"

"I understand," the teen responded.

"Nick," Lisa said, grabbing him by the arm, "have them check at the hospital and in my office." Then she turned to the lieutenant. "She comes there to see me quite often, and she knows the place like the back of her hand. It's a kid thing, you know."

"Understood, ma'am. We'll check it out."

Lisa watched her son leave with the soldiers and then went back into the house and attempted to contact Paul but found her phone was still blocked from calling the space station or anywhere else except the hospital. While the authorities were allowing the hospital staff to consult with Lisa about her patients, Lisa knew they were monitoring all her calls, and anything beyond that exclusive purpose was prohibited.

While the United States' attempt to launch its nukes at the moon had failed, the Russians managed a successful launch from their Baikonur Cosmodrome. While tensions between the United States and Russia were still volatile, there was enough goodwill remaining between the respective space programs to keep the lines of communication open. Given the considerable angst the aliens were causing all the militaries worldwide, there was a willingness to work together to solve the problem. It was on this basis that the Russians informed the Americans of their successful launch. It also gave them a great opportunity to claim their program was superior.

Lisa had been completely wrong in telling the lieutenant of Rianne's possible whereabouts. After checking out the girl's school and the hospital, she was nowhere to be found. The lieutenant gathered her personnel and strategized: some would knock on nearby doors with Nick, while the lieutenant would question Lisa about other relatives or friends with whom Rianne might be hiding. Canine units would also be deployed to help in the search effort.

Rianne's initial instinct after she caught up to Ralph, was to go back to her parent's house, but after further consideration she thought better of it. She thought about going to her grandmother's or her aunt Becca's, but something told her this might also be risky. She assumed that if she was going to be a fugitive on the run, she would have to hide where no one expected her to be, especially her mom. While she had no desire to worry her mom, she also realized that her freedom was a valuable commodity under the circumstances, and out of concern for her, Lisa might give Rianne's usual haunts away. Other than a few dollars her mom had stuck in her pocket just days prior, she had no other belongings with her. But she had her dog, and the weather was warm, so what else did a girl possibly need?

However, while it might have been possible for her to avoid being caught if she were on her own, the dog proved to be a major problem, especially with the military canines tracking them. Ralph was an adorable dog and a good friend, but he was not the most disciplined animal, and as a result Rianne's progress toward getting far away from home was considerably impeded. By the early evening, Rianne was back in custody.

The lieutenant notified the general of the capture immediately and fully expected to be told to take the girl home straightaway. But Tillard took the view that having the girl detained could provide critical leverage if for some reason the Russian rocket now hurtling toward the moon should be unsuccessful in its mission. On that basis he ordered the lieutenant to bring the young girl to their headquarters at Ellington Field Joint Reserve Base near Houston where they would arrange to hold her under the pretext of needing to protect her from trying to escape again. Although all of this was supposedly being done for Rianne's own protection, the lieutenant was told not to tell Lisa that they found her daughter. While the lieutenant had little choice but to follow the general's orders, as a mother, she in no way condoned what she was being required to do.

"What do you mean you can't find her?" Lisa shouted, chastising the young lieutenant. "She can't have gotten far."

"We checked everywhere you suggested, Dr. Franklin. The school, the hospital. No one's seen her. Even your son couldn't find her."

Nick just looked at his mother and shrugged.

Lisa turned back to the lieutenant. "How about the friends I told you about."

"Nothing, ma'am."

"Well, then I need to go and look for her myself," Lisa said as she moved to grab her keys and purse.

"I can't let you do that, Dr. Franklin."

"On whose authority?" Lisa fumed.

"General Tillard, ma'am."

"Then at least let me call my husband," she pleaded.

"I can't, ma'am. General's orders."

"Screw the general!" Nick yelled as he rose up from the chair on which he was sprawled and bolted for his room. Lisa watched him leave, feeling like her entire family was disintegrating before her eyes.

"Sorry, ma'am.

"Whom can I talk to?" Lisa implored. "There must be somebody."

"I'm not sure, ma'am. But I'll talk to the general and ask."

An hour later Rianne was chaperoned by the lieutenant to the general's office, was given something to drink and a few snacks, and then asked to sit down and wait for the general. The lieutenant had supplied the girl with some rope as a leash for the dog so Rianne was at least happy that her four-legged friend remained with her. Rianne worried about her mother, aware that Lisa was probably worried sick, but Rianne figured that she would be going home soon. In fact, she was surprised they didn't just take her there to begin with.

The general emerged from his inner office just minutes after the girl arrived and asked Rianne to join him inside. Rianne entered the office and sat in a leather chair on the opposite side of the general's desk, with Ralph jumping into the chair beside her, which made Rianne feel slightly more at ease. The female lieutenant remained just inside the general's office door.

The general closed the office door, sat behind the desk, and then took time to make a personal assessment of the girl who sat before him. After a minute or so, he finally spoke.

"You're name is Rianne, is that right?"

"Yes, sir.

"I understand you were the one who first discovered the aliens on the moon." His tone of voice was warm and fatherly.

"Yes, sir," the girl said politely, not yet sure whether the general was a friend or foe.

"That's quite a feather in your cap, wouldn't you say?"

"I was really just lucky, sir. That's all."

"Oh, come on, you can take more credit than that. Not many people would have paid close attention like you did or would know when something like that happening on the moon was out of place."

"I only know because my dad taught me. He's an astronaut onboard the space station."

"I am aware of that," the general said, smiling through a touch of egotism.

"I figured," the girl replied. "I was just making conversation. My mom told me that was a polite thing to do."

"Of course," the general replied, trying his best to hide his irritation. "Have you met the aliens?" he continued, probing for any additional information he could get.

"I've been to the moon. Or at least, my mind has been to the moon."

"How does that work, if you don't mind my asking?"

"I have no idea, but it was pretty cool."

"Cool, huh?" the general said with a patronizing smile.

"Yes, sir. I got a chance to see my father."

"Did you meet Entity? Your dad's friend."

"No, sir. I just talked to my father. I never met Entity."

"Then how do you know you were on the moon? Maybe it was just a dream."

"It was no dream, sir. I even saw a building change, right in front of my eyes."

"Really? These aliens must be pretty powerful?"

"Yes, sir. I think they must be."

The general rose and walked to the front of his desk, leaning against the edge directly in front of the girl. "Rianne, we're trying to get your father to help us stop the aliens."

"Are they doing something wrong?" the girl interrupted.

"They're taking away our weapons. Taking away our ability to defend ourselves."

"But if nobody has any weapons, doesn't that mean no one will have so much to worry about?"

"In a perfect world, Rianne, that might be the case. But the world isn't perfect, and the aliens are putting us in grave danger. And your dad is helping them do it."

"My dad wouldn't do anything to hurt anyone."

"Not on purpose. But the aliens may be exerting some kind of mind control on him, like they did to you when they brought you up to the moon. He might not know what's happening to him and, by accident, end up hurting people here on Earth. You wouldn't want his actions to put your mom's life in danger, would you?"

"No, sir."

"I didn't think so," the general said as he leaned back a little, taking another moment to assess the girl's loyalties. "Suppose I were to let you call your father and talk to him. Perhaps you could persuade him to help us stop the aliens before they destroy us."

"How would he do that?"

"By getting inside Entity's head. By trying to find out how they do what they do. By identifying their power source; any information that would be helpful in exposing their vulnerabilities. Your dad is the only person those aliens are talking to, and we need him to be on our side."

"But he is on our side."

"Then it should be easy to convince him to help." The general waited a moment and then leaned forward and handed the girl the cell phone sitting on his desk. "Call him. I've given orders to allow the call to go through."

Rianne took the phone and then took in the man who was sitting in front of her. She didn't feel that the general was a bad man, but Rianne did feel the general was mistaken in his perception of her father. She glanced back toward the lieutenant, but the lieutenant remained passive. The youngster debated in her head whether she should do what she had been asked or whether she should turn down the offer. But it had been so long since she had talked to her dad that it was impossible to turn down the opportunity. However, she had no idea what she would say. With great trepidation she keyed in the number with the general's eyes fixed upon her. Paul answered on the second ring.

"Yes, General," Paul said in a voice with a distinct edge.

"Hi, Dad," Rianne said with a shaky voice, waiting expectantly, knowing her father would be surprised.

"Ri? Is that you?" Paul said, clearly baffled.

"It's me, Dad."

"What are you doing on the general's phone?"

The general reached out and put the cell on speakerphone. Then he handed it back to the girl.

"I asked Rianne to call you, Paul," the general said. "I think she has something she wants to ask you."

"Rianne, where are you?"

"I'm in the general's office."

"How did you get there?" Paul asked, both angry and worried.

"I had to chase Ralph down. He ran out of our yard through the fence, and some soldiers picked me up and brought me here."

"Does your mother know where you are?"

"No. I don't think so."

"Are they going to take you home?"

"I don't know, Dad," the girl said, looking directly at the general.

"She's safe with us, Paul. We won't let anything happen to her."

"I can't believe you would do this, General."

"Do what?" the general replied innocently.

"Use a child as a pawn."

"We are doing no such thing. Rianne just wanted to talk to you."

"I'd call it kidnapping," Paul snapped.

"You can call it anything you want. I call it a matter of national security," the general fired back.

"The general wanted me to ask you to cooperate with the army, Dad. So they can stop the aliens. He said the aliens were going to destroy the world and you need to help defeat them."

"Is that what you think I should do, Ri? What would you recommend I do?"

The girl looked at the general, thought for a moment, and then said "I don't think you should listen to the general, Dad. I think he's wrong."

"Give me that," the general said, ripping the cell phone from the girl's hand. "I was hoping to get your daughter to talk some sense into you, but I can see that was a mistake. I should have known."

"You better get her back to her mother, General, or else—"

"Or else what, Connors?" The general seethed. "You're not exactly in a position to demand much of anything at the moment."

"I can't believe you're using my daughter like this."

"The entire world is at stake, Connors. Under the circumstances I will do whatever is necessary to save it. I want the world back, and you want your daughter back. So what are you willing to do to help me?"

"What do you want me to do?" Paul asked, his voice low and menacing.

"I want you to cozy up to your friend Entity. Use your relationship to get as much information as you can. The Russians have a rocket with a payload of nukes on their way up to the moon, and it should be there in a day or so. But just in case it doesn't wipe them out, you will provide us with a backup plan."

"Don't do it, Dad!" Rianne shouted. "Stick to your guns. For me." The girl looked right into the general's eyes. "I think those are the only kind of guns we should stick to."

"The choice is yours, Connors," the general said, ignoring the girl's comment. "I'm not bluffing. I'll be sticking to my guns as well." The general ended the call and stared at Rianne with an air of disapproval. "That was a foolish thing to do, young lady. You may not understand, but one day you will. We're just trying to do what's necessary."

"I think that's what the aliens are trying to do too, sir."

"You don't really know what the aliens are trying to do, Rianne. No one really knows."

"My dad knows."

"Your dad *thinks* he knows. What if he's wrong?"

"What if he's right?"

"There is no right in this situation, my dear. Only wrong, and we need to stop it."

"Then can I go home now?"

"No, I don't think so. Not quite yet."

Rianne looked at Ralph, who licked her face as if to say everything will be all right. The general rose and walked to the door. Rianne could hear him talking quietly to the lieutenant in the outer office, telling her to "Secure quarters for the girl until further notice."

Lisa slept very little that night, sick with worry about Rianne. While she knew her daughter was very resourceful, she was aware that the forces aligned against her daughter were formidable. Lisa thought about something to eat but simply lacked the energy or appetite to do so. Then her cell phone rang.

"Hello," Lisa said, hoping to hear her daughter's voice.

"Lisa, this is Ken."

"Ken! Thank God. It's so good to hear from you. You have no idea what's been going on."

"I have an inkling. It's hard to conceal everything from Galaxy since we're so intertwined with space-station operations."

"Do you know where Rianne is?" Lisa asked with great desperation in her voice.

"I don't know for sure, but I suspect that the military has her in custody. General Tillard contacted me and requested I call you. He indicated that one of his lieutenants told you she would ask if there was anyone you could talk to. I guess you're stuck with me."

"I'll have to thank that young lieutenant." Lisa paused a moment and then proceeded in a hushed tone. "What's going on, Ken? Why are they doing this?"

"I think they're using Rianne to force Paul to help them undermine the alien agenda. As near as I can tell, the military is unnerved by across-the-board-system failures they're encountering. Apparently when the aliens were talking about getting rid of guns, they were also including bombs, missiles, ships, planes, knives, and anything else that can cause havoc in the hands of those intent on doing harm. The country's preparedness has already been degraded to less than fifty percent of what it was formerly."

"My God," Lisa said, startled, but amazed. "Are we in danger?"

"The military seems to think so, but in point of fact, all the military systems planet-wide are being subjected to the same restraints. This step-down is being accomplished in a highly coordinated and ostensibly orderly manner, and so far no one has found a way to stop it."

"Ken, I need to talk to Paul. He needs to know what's happened to Rianne."

"Lisa, I doubt that the general will allow that. Besides, if I'm right about why they're keeping Rianne, I would bet that Entity has already told Paul. But I need to call him on another matter, and I'll try my best to verify that he has the message."

"Thanks, Ken. And tell him I love him."

"I'll do what I can."

The call ended.

It was an odd juxtaposition that Paul found himself in during this whole alien affair. He had always wanted to be an astronaut, but if anyone had told him he would be a central figure in humankind's first encounter with an alien life form and, what's more, would be the spokesperson for those aliens, he would have told the person that he or she was crazy! Yet he still had some lingering doubts as to whether he was doing the right thing by siding with the aliens. But the more he watched the escalating tensions grow and realized that most of the threats were coming from Earth, the more convinced he became that his choice was the appropriate one. More than that, he was coming to the conclusion that the aliens were right in that it was the only choice if humankind was to survive.

That evening Ken Ishida called Paul on a disposable burner phone he picked up. Though he was the mission commander for Galaxy Enterprises, he was aware that even his calls were now probably subject to monitoring. Things had deteriorated so much that he was starting to feel like he was living in the old Soviet Union rather than the United States.

"I take it you know what's been going on down here?" Ken asked the astronaut.

"I know that Tillard is holding Rianne, and I know the Russians have a rocket on the way to the moon." Paul was no longer worried about being monitored. At this juncture there seemed to be little more that anyone could do to hurt him. He joked, "Something tells me that Tillard doesn't like me very much."

"Something tells me you're right, Paul. It's a good thing you're a civilian astronaut."

"Roger that."

"Are you worried about the nukes headed to the moon?" Ken continued.

"Not much I can do about it, but I will do my best to tell Entity. Of course they probably know already."

"Do you think they're in danger?" Ken asked with mixed feelings.

"I don't know. I know they have capabilities beyond our comprehension, but how far they extend, I simply have no idea."

"Well, if they should survive the attack, I have a network and a well-known anchor who is looking forward to interviewing you."

"Who is it?" Paul inquired.

"I'd rather not say, just in case this call is somehow being monitored. I'm calling on a disposable phone, but out of caution, let's just keep them guessing. I won't give you a definitive time, but I will say I think you should be ready over the next couple of days. I have given them permission to videoconference. I think it's important for everyone to see your face."

"Why?" Paul asked, laughing.

"It's honest looking. Besides, it will focus their attention."

"Thanks, Ken. For everything. Watching my family, supporting me, facilitating."

"We'll see when this is over whether I deserve your thanks or not. For the moment, we seem to be in this together."

"Semper fi, buddy."

"Semper fi, my friend. Good luck."

"Why did you want to see us tonight?" Entity asked Paul as the alien emerged from the fog.

"You mean you don't already know?"

"Well, you could be worried about your daughter or your son or your wife," Entity suggested. "Or you could be worried about the warheads that are coming toward the moon. You could also be worried about the fate of your planet or whether you have done the right thing in regard to us, as those thoughts seem to be cropping up occasionally in your mind to this day. It could be any one of these things or a million others."

"I think you've covered it all, though I'm not really questioning my judgment about you as much these days. Being on the space station has always been good for enhancing one's perspective, and my involvement with you has only reinforced that view. I think humankind needs help. I only hope you can deliver."

"We understand. But first things first."

"Dad!"

Paul heard Rianne's voice first, followed by a bark, and then saw his daughter emerge from the bank of fog, quickly followed by Ralph. As soon as Rianne saw her father standing there, she ran to him and threw her arms around him.

"I love you, Daddy."

"I love you too, sweetheart."

"This is Ralph, Dad." Rianne took a step back to make the introduction. "He's my good friend."

"Hello, Ralph." Paul smiled and leaned down and shook the paw that was being offered to him, and then he patted the dog on the head.

"He likes you, Dad."

"I like him too." After another pat, Paul turned his attention to his daughter. "Are they treating you all right, Rianne?" Paul asked with genuine concern and affection.

"They were a little scary at first, but they're all right. Ralph is with me, and they put a gaming system in the room so I have something to play with. I'm just worried about Mom because she doesn't know where I am."

"But I do, Ri."

Rianne turned in the direction of the next familiar voice she heard and saw her mother coming out of the fog. Lisa stood in front of her, relieved that Rianne was all right. "It's so good to see you, Ri. And you too, Ralph," she said as she stroked the dog's head.

"It's good to see you too, Mom. I was worried about you worrying about me, but Ralph and I are doing fine."

"And I'm happy to see you too, Paul. I feel like I'm cheating, but I'm past the point of caring." The two embraced and then took their daughter into the fold.

"Thank you," Paul said, turning to the alien.

"We're the ones who are thankful" Entity replied.

"I'd introduce you," Paul offered, indicating his wife and daughter, "but I'm pretty sure you know who these people are already."

"We thought about bringing your son, Nick, here to join you as well," Entity said apologetically, "but he is so full of negative thoughts right now we thought it might be unwise."

"We understand," Paul acknowledged. "But we love him nonetheless."

"Of course."

"Perhaps some time in the future," Lisa offered.

"Perhaps," said the entity softly.

"You're truly magical, you know that?" Lisa said to Entity, Lisa's eyes welling up with tears.

"Not magic. A simple interface," was Entity's humble explanation.

"Well, it's magic to us," said Lisa, "and we are forever grateful.

"We are," Paul agreed, "but at the moment I'm a little worried about us being here. What about the Russian rocket?" Paul inquired. "Does your magic extend that far?"

"The rocket was actually something we allowed to launch," Entity explained. "When Rianne first observed us on the moon's surface, we were setting up a photon collector to capture your sun's rays while we set up operations on the backside of your moon. We will actually detonate the warheads before they strike the moon and absorb the energy they produce. They pose no threat and will provide power to part of our systems."

"Why didn't you do that with the American rocket?" Paul inquired, appearing slightly offended.

"It had more energy than we required, whereas the Russian rocket has a more compatible output. It was simply more suitable to our needs and will not cause any damage."

"I should have guessed," Paul admitted, a bit embarrassed, and somewhat awestruck.

"Everything is fine, and I am going to send everyone back now, except for you, Paul. We need to talk about the interview that will be taking place the day after tomorrow."

"Good to know," said Paul with a laugh. He kissed his wife and daughter goodbye, patted Ralph one more time, and then glanced at Entity. By the time he looked back toward Lisa, Rianne, and the dog, they were gone. He turned back to Entity and said, "So what do you think I should say in the interview?"

"Whatever you think best. We trust you will represent us favorably."

"Then can I ask you a few questions?"

"I would be happy to answer what I can," Entity said as they walked and talked.

The next morning General Tillard received an urgent call from the lieutenant, informing him that their young hostage could not be awakened and appeared to be in a coma. His staff had tried everything, including shaking, talking, slapping, and even spraying cold water, but nothing was working. Rianne was carted over to the base dispensary, but none of the doctors there met with any success either.

It didn't take long for the general to realize the potential risk this posed in the way of bad press. While his people had done nothing to hurt the girl, the detention of a preteen female under questionable circumstances was not going to sit well with the general public, even in these extremely stressful times. He ordered his staff to have the girl taken to the hospital where Lisa worked and to notify Rianne's mother immediately. When he got off the phone, he could only hope that his strategy had not blown up in his face.

The world watched with great anticipation as the Russian rocket neared the moon. No one knew how the Russian scientists had managed to launch the rocket and evade the fate that other nations' weapons systems had succumbed to. All that mattered was that people seemed happy that someone had succeeded and that an end to the world's alien nightmare might be near.

The Russians continued to be rather smug about their accomplishment, but little did they know that the aliens had seized upon the opportunity to tap the power that was being served up to them. As the rocket approached the moon, crowds formed all over the planet to see if they could catch a glimpse of the event as it unfolded. News broadcasts claimed that it was unlikely that people would see much of anything since the explosions would be taking place on the far side of the moon, but they added that it might be possible to see some afterglow, warning that people should protect their eyes should anything happen, such as a premature detonation that might bring the explosions into view.

As it happened the whole thing turned out to be a nonevent. The explosions did take place but were not visible, nor did the warheads impact the surface of the moon. It wasn't long before Earth's scientists speculated that it was the aliens who controlled the entire situation, and soon after morale around the globe plummeted even further on the news.

As soon as the call from the general's office had ended, Lisa alerted Nick that Rianne had been found, at which point Nick insisted he go with Lisa to the hospital. Lisa wasn't sure if Nick's anger toward her over McKenzie's death had abated somewhat or whether he was coming with Lisa to make sure she didn't kill his sister as well, but either way she was happy to have him tag along. The more time they spent together, the more likely their relationship would mend quickly. At least that was what Lisa hoped would happen.

As she drove to the hospital, she was confident that she knew exactly what was going on, that her daughter was just fine but had yet to wake from her moon visit, but there was a part of Lisa that felt the need for a little payback when it came to the general. What he had done was outrageous, and anything she did to inflict some measure of guilt and uncertainty into his life for a short time was called for as far as Lisa was concerned.

It had been days since Lisa was at the hospital, but it took only seconds for her to feel like she was back in the swing of things. Rianne was in the emergency room, with curtains drawn and a team of panicked doctors trying to revive her. When Lisa got there, she looked over Rianne's chart and then requested the doctors to leave her alone with her daughter. As soon as they did, she pulled the curtains shut and sat down with Nick and simply waited. Within the hour Rianne was awake and smiling.

"Are you okay?" she asked her daughter, already certain of her answer.

"I'm fine, Mom," the girl responded. "It was so nice to see Dad."

"Yes, it was," Lisa agreed wholeheartedly.

"What does she mean it was nice to see Dad?" Nick demanded to know.

"I'll fill you in later," Lisa told him, hoping to avoid a scene at the hospital.

"Hi, Nick," Rianne said, waving at her brother.

"Hey, punk," her brother responded almost affectionately. "I never thought I'd say it, but it's good to see you."

Watching her two kids sparring playfully lifted Lisa's spirits some, but she sensed that there were doctors who were still nearby just outside the thin curtains. She needed to communicate what she planned to do next, so she spoke very softly, directly into Rianne's ear. "I am going to have them keep you in the hospital for observation."

"But I feel great, Mom. Really," the girl whispered.

"I know, Ri. But this will hopefully give me some leverage to leave the house so I can know what's going on. And you'll get to watch television and maybe even see your dad's interview. I promise it will only be for a day or two."

"What interview?" Nick asked out loud, feeling totally left out of the loop.

"I told you I'll fill you in later," Lisa whispered, shushing him with a finger to her lips.

"Fine. You do that," the young man said as he left the area in a huff for parts unknown.

"He hates me," Lisa said to her daughter glumly.

"He hates everybody, Mom. He's a teenager."

"Great. You'll be a teenager shortly too. Is that how you'll be?

"Probably. It comes with the territory," Rianne said gleefully. "Bet you can't wait, huh?"

"Oh, absolutely. Can't wait," Lisa sighed.

"What about Ralph?" asked Rianne, obviously concerned.

"I'll get Ralph. Don't you worry. I'll need protection since you won't be around. Especially from my son."

"Thanks, Mom."

Lisa kissed her daughter on the forehead and then pulled the curtain back, handing Rianne's chart to one of the physicians who had been treating her originally.

"We tried everything," the resident said. "We thought she was in a coma. What did you do to bring her out of it?"

"A mother's secret," Lisa said, smiling. "But I think she should stay here for a day or two just to make sure we haven't missed anything."

"Of course," said the resident, who was clearly dumfounded by the entire experience.

Lisa wished that she could explain what had happened and reassure her fellow doctors that it was the aliens and that they were nothing to fear, but that was something she was going to have to leave for her husband.

Lisa went back one last time to say goodbye to Rianne and then went up to check on a few of her patients who were still at the hospital. Afterwards she stopped at her office to see how much work had piled up while she had been confined to home. She found her desk buried, which was not a surprise, but vowed to make the general feel the pain along with her. As she was ruminating about all the evil things she wanted to do, there was a gentle knock on her door.

"Ma'am," a semi familiar voice called out. Lisa turned and found the pretty young lieutenant standing there, lid in hand.

"How did you find me?" Lisa asked, a little worried that the lieutenant was about to put her back in custody.

"One of the doctors in the emergency room directed me here. The general wanted to know how your daughter is."

"She seems to be fine, no thanks to the general. But we are going to keep her here for a day or two to make sure she's not in any danger."

"Do you know what happened?"

"We think the aliens took her," Lisa quipped, unable to stop herself.

"You're kidding, right, ma'am?" the lieutenant asked a little uneasily.

"Of course I'm kidding." Lisa surmised from the expression on the lieutenant's face that generals tend to drain the humor from their junior officers. "It could just be a kid thing," Lisa said, letting her off the hook. "If we don't see anything in a day or two, we'll send her home. But until then, as an attending physician at this hospital, I request that I be allowed to treat my daughter."

"That sounds reasonable, Dr. Connors. I'll let the general know. I'm sure he'll be relieved to hear your daughter's okay."

"I'll bet." The lieutenant turned to leave. "By the way," Lisa said, stopping her momentarily, "I owe you a thanks for speaking to the general on my behalf."

"For what, ma'am?"

"You got me someone to talk to. It's something I really needed at the time. Thanks."

"Oh, that. You're welcome, ma'am. Glad to do it."

"And could you ask the general to get our dog back to the house?"

"I'll do that, ma'am. In fact, I'll do that myself. He's a nice dog."

"Thanks, Lieutenant."

"And, ma'am, I thought the general was wrong."

"Thanks," Lisa said, smiling through her mother's pain.

With that the young officer departed, and Lisa began digging into the pile of papers infiltrating her space. She had only been working a minute or two when someone else came by her door.

"Mom."

Lisa recognized Nick's voice immediately and turned her chair toward her son. He looked so tall and handsome, but his eyes were full of tears. "I'm sorry, Mom. I know you did everything you could for McKenzie. I'm sorry."

Lisa went right to Nick and wrapped her arms around him as he sobbed, his head resting on her shoulder. She didn't know what to say, but she thanked God for her son's forgiveness. What he had gone through was something that no student, no child, foreign or domestic, should ever have to witness, and in that moment her heart went out to all the children of the world.

Paul was fully back onboard the ISS and looking over the Onboard Short Term Plan Viewer when the call came through. Paul never considered himself much of a public speaker, and a part of him was dreading the call. His conversation with Entity the night before had been far more detailed than previous discussions, but even though he now had more information, he still felt like he had no idea of what he would ultimately say. The fact that he didn't know whom he would be speaking to or what questions would be asked did not help bolster his confidence either.

Paul felt somewhat relieved to discover that the interview would be taking place at Galaxy's headquarters and that Ken Ishida would be at the journalist's side. The interviewer was a woman named Naomi Roberts. While she had no background as a scientist, she was a respected television journalist, which Ken felt would be important under the current circumstances with public trust at an all-time low. Paul worried that he would be unable to answer Naomi's questions given his limited understanding of the aliens' science. But having watched Naomi on television many times, he knew her to be a down-to-earth individual who seemed relatively easy to talk to. Additionally, the interview was being taped, so there was less chance of it being blacked out by stations, as it might be had it been live.

Ken made the introductions although not much was needed. Both participants were well known to the general public, and each recognized the other. Naomi then officially began the interview.

"I suppose I should ask you how you are doing. I understand that you're on an extended mission to study the effects of zero G on the human body."

"That's true."

"How's that going?" Naomi asked cordially.

"It's going well. I'll be losing my crewmate, Martina Giammani, shortly, but there will be some new crew members coming onboard in a few weeks."

"I apologize for not remembering, but how long is your mission scheduled to last?"

"A minimum of a year and a half, and more if I can muster the courage."

Naomi smiled. "You must miss your family."

"I do, and I don't," Paul said, putting some thought behind it. "In fact it's odd you should say that." He decided he would use her comment to steer the conversation toward its inevitable heart.

"Why is that?"

"Because the purpose of a long-duration mission is to simulate a flight to Mars, which would include studying both psychological and physiological effects. But on the former subject, I've had a chance to cheat."

"Can you explain?"

"I wish I could. I just know that it happened. I saw my wife and my daughter quite recently. I even met our new dog, Ralph."

Naomi had a quizzical look on her face, almost like she was convinced she was being tested in terms of what she was willing to believe. "What about your son? Don't you have a teenage boy as well?"

"Yes. But he wasn't invited, so to speak."

"Why not?"

"It's a long story, and somewhat personal, and I'd really rather not go there if that's all right."

"That's fine." Naomi sensed Paul's feelings were genuine and decided to let it go. Besides, there were always alternative ways of uncovering information.

"So you saw your wife and your daughter recently."

"And the dog," Ken interjected from the side.

"Where was this?" Naomi asked with a hint of skepticism, ignoring Ken's comment completely.

"On the moon." Paul knew that this was a bombshell and gave Naomi a moment to absorb what he had just said.

"How could that be?" the woman asked, clearly having a difficult time taking this in.

"As I said before, I don't know, but it definitely happened, on several occasions. What the mechanism is, I couldn't begin to tell you."

"What *can* you tell us?"

"I can tell you that there is an unbelievably advanced race that has set up temporary residence on the moon."

"How many of them are there?" the woman asked, her voice betraying a modicum of fear.

"I don't know if there are any of them there," was Paul's honest response.

"I'm sorry, Mr. Connors, but you've lost me."

"I'm not trying to be obtuse. I can only relate what I know. I communicate with an entity who has adopted that very name."

"Entity?"

"Yes. It is an ephemeral being who looks vaguely like my wife who first made contact with me while I've been aboard the International Space Station."

"How was this contact made?"

"I'm not sure. Generally my physical body remains aboard the space station sleeping, but my consciousness is somehow transferred to the moon, a building, or buildings they set up, more for me, I think, than for themselves. I also believe their energy source is housed there. They have somehow found a way to create something like wormholes and place them wherever needed."

Naomi, whose only knowledge of wormholes came from science-fiction movies, brushed Paul's assertion aside without a second thought and continued on. "Why contact you, do you think? Because you're an astronaut? Because you're on the space station?"

"I think those factors may play into it, but I think there are other more significant, tangible reasons."

"Such as?"

"It was my daughter who discovered their presence. She was looking at the moon through a telescope I bought for her so she could view the space station. Anyway, she took a video of what she saw, and I showed that video to my superiors. However, later I came to understand that they had been interested in me specifically."

"Was there some special reason?"

"Yes, it would seem I am less than perfect," Paul said with a self-deprecating smile, "but they view me as honest. And I think they knew how I felt about guns."

"How *do* you feel about them?" the reporter inquired.

"I've kind of left them behind."

"You don't like guns?"

"Not much. Not anymore."

"I don't understand. How could this entity know that?"

"Oh, they know a lot, believe me. They try to know what's on everybody's mind. They certainly know what's on mine."

"So you're saying you don't believe in guns or the Second Amendment and this is why they chose you?"

"I never said anything about the Second Amendment, so I need to clarify something. I fully support the Second Amendment, as it was originally framed."

"But you don't think it applies today?"

"It still applies as it pertains to the society we live in, where there is violence all around us and people feel the need to protect themselves, but the aliens' goal is to change that paradigm. Besides, at this point, whether I believe in it or not is a moot point, because they're intent on changing all that in any case."

"And you're all right with that?"

"I wasn't at first, but I am now."

"Why?"

"Let's just say that I got to a place where I saw no point in trying to fight it. I've moved on to—acceptance."

"It sounds like death and dying."

"Or maybe rebirth."

Naomi paused for a moment, trying to feel Paul out, a little unsure about what to ask next. Finally she said, "I understand that you were a former Marine? A decorated one at that."

"I am. Not even former. Once a Marine, always a Marine."

"I wouldn't have thought a Marine such as yourself would have given up so easily."

Paul could feel a little hostility creeping into his intended answer and did his best to stifle it. "No Marine gives up easily, and I certainly wouldn't be on the space station if I gave up easily. But I came to see the senselessness of killing firsthand and the way it changes people and society. It certainly changed me."

"But as you said, you're onboard the space station. You must have passed a battery of psychological tests to get there, which means somebody thinks you're pretty well adjusted."

"I probably am. But I'm far from perfect."

"That would be an unrealistically high bar to set for yourself in any case, don't you think?"

"Perhaps. But there's nothing wrong with trying to shoot for the moon. Unfortunately for me, however, I can never achieve it—perfection. It's like the speed of light; I can't even come close."

"So what? None of us is perfect," the woman reflected.

"Yes. But some of us are even less so," Paul said sadly, as though he were in a confessional. "When I was in the Marines, I killed someone whom, even at the time, I feared should not have been killed."

"Then why did you do it?" Naomi said gently.

"Because he was threatening a fellow Marine."

"Then you were just doing your job."

"Yes. That was the problem. My job, my duty, was to protect my fellow Marines, but he had just attempted to assault this poor man's daughter, and the man was trying to protect his family. It all happened very quickly, and I just reacted, but in looking back I knew it was wrong and thought there had to be another answer, another way of dealing with the situation."

"Did you ever find one?"

"Of a sort. I reasoned that if I hadn't joined the Marines, and if I didn't have a gun, that man would still be alive."

"But then that Marine might be dead," Naomi offered, "although I certainly don't approve of what you say he did."

"Yes. It's a conundrum at best. In any case, I left a young girl not much older than my daughter with a dead father. I thought to bring charges against that Marine after we returned to base, but he was killed by an IED before I ever got the chance. I eventually went back to where it all happened, but I was never able to find that girl." Paul went silent for a second, the pain of the situation clearly evident, and then spoke again. "When my enlistment was up, I left the Marines, I got rid of my guns, and I tried to raise my boy in such a way that he might never find himself in a similar situation."

"You're aware that there's no way you could predict your son's future. There is no way you can really protect your son from everything. Life just happens."

"I would agree, that is until I met Entity. How could I resist supporting the idea of a world free of weapons and violence?"

"How would that even be possible?"

"Once again, I can't answer that question. But from what I can see, it's happening nonetheless."

"So you are affirming that it is the aliens who are responsible for the current crisis?"

"Without a doubt, though I'm not sure I agree with that description."

"What gives them the right to do all this without asking first?"

"I think these aliens knew what our answer would be from the beginning and they didn't feel they could accept it. They knew what was happening on Earth long before they got here, just by watching and listening to our electronic mediums. Our news. Our entertainment. Everything. They had formed an opinion of where it was all heading, and they didn't want to be culpable for what would probably happen."

"But what gives them the right to decide for us?" Naomi persisted.

"Experience maybe. These are beings that are ostensibly millions of years older and more advanced than we are. And they respect us, and value us, and feel it imperative that they help ensure our survival. From their vantage point, they see us, and in fact all intelligent life, as unique and worthy of preservation. And they see only one thing standing in the way of that happening as it pertains to us, our tendency to solve our problems through violence and war. If they remove the means of facilitating violence, wherever it might rear its ugly head, and if they can give human beings a few generations free from violence, it might wash it from our systems. Reboot our DNA as it were."

"We're not all that bad," Naomi said somewhat defensively.

"Really? You really believe that?" Paul said with a strong dose of sarcasm.

"I hope that," Naomi said, acknowledging some small bit of disappointment with her world. "But we are a free society, and we should be free to make our own choices, not have someone dictating the terms to us."

"I don't remember God giving us a choice about the Ten Commandments," Paul stated rather abruptly, surprising even himself. "He just put it in writing and said do it. I'm not sure I see much difference here."

Naomi smiled, almost amused by Paul's seeming arrogance. "Are you likening these aliens to God?"

"I wouldn't presume, but there are parallels. And I have to ask myself, what are we afraid of? As a race we've tried to change ourselves and be less violent, but it has yet to work. They are offering us a way out."

"By taking away the means."

"Precisely," Paul shot back.

"To let that happen would require an implausible leap of faith on our part, don't you think?"

"Without a doubt. But I can tell you from what limited time I've spent with Entity, that it could be wonderful. There is such a feeling of serenity in their presence."

"I can vouch for that," Ken stated out of the blue.

"You've met Entity?" Naomi asked Ken.

"No. But Entity brought me to the moon and let me experience what Paul is talking about. It was that experience that had me seek you out."

"It's not the weapons the aliens want to rid us of," Paul explained. "It's the instinct, the desire to kill."

"But killing is part of the life cycle. We wouldn't exist without it," Naomi countered.

"And Entity wouldn't argue with that," Paul agreed. "But there is that which is necessary for survival, and there is killing that is done for revenge or sport or war, or whatever. That is what they see as destroying us."

"Well, it all sounds rather utopian, but perhaps that's just me," Naomi said, sending a clear signal that the interview was near its end as far as she was concerned. "Is there anything more you'd like to add before we wrap this up?"

Paul sensed he had lost her and was desperate to know how he could make his case. "Only that I have felt conflicted over this whole affair from the beginning." He paused yet again, struggling to put his feelings into words. "In all fairness, at one point Entity told me point-blank they would stop what they were doing if I really felt they should."

"And you didn't?" Naomi asked, so taken aback that she totally stopped what she was doing.

"I couldn't. I dreamed once that I told them to leave, and then I turned on the news. And everything had gone back to the way it was. School shootings, stabbings, trucks running people over, gas attacks, rapes, and kidnappings. Threats of war. I woke up in a cold sweat, praying the aliens were still there. And they were. I just couldn't be responsible for denying humankind of what they were offering. It would be like," he struggled a moment, searching for the right example, "denying people of the joy of having children. How could I live with that on my conscience?"

"But to make that kind of monumental decision for everyone—" Naomi pressed.

"Those were the only alternatives I was offered," Paul responded. "Given that choice, it seemed to me the only thing I could do."

Naomi looked at Paul for a moment, pondering what he had said. "I don't know if this interview is going to quell any fears or change people's opinions, but you've certainly given people something to think about. I don't know what their final verdict will be once they hear this. But I know I can certainly state unequivocally, I wouldn't want to be in your shoes. Too much responsibility." She paused, and when she started to speak again, her tone softened noticeably. "I wish you success on your mission, and I pray your decision was the right one. For all of us."

"Roger that," said Paul with a smile.

"Goodbye, Mr. Connors.

"Goodbye, Ms. Roberts."

"I'll be in touch later, Paul," Ken said before the screen went to Galaxy's logo.

After the interview ended, Naomi sat quietly for several seconds before turning to Ken. She had done a lot of interviews over the course of her career, but she had never experienced anything as profound as this, with so many ambiguities and ethical issues, not to mention economic ones, impacting the entirety of the human race.

"You look drained," Ken remarked, in part to cover her silence.

"I don't know what to say. Part of me feels what they are doing is wrong, yet I am almost sure that given the same situation I would feel compelled to make the same choices Paul Connors has made. I suppose what I am really feeling is fear."

"Of the unknown?" asked Ken.

"Of peace. Am I really afraid of peace?"

Paul sat quietly in his CQ, trying to assess how he had done. He wished he could call his family, and technically he probably could have, but he was still unaware of how the situation had changed for his family back on Earth. His mind kept going through all the things he did say, should have said, or could have said, finally deciding that it was just better not to think of it at all. He went over his assignments on the Onboard Short Term Plan Viewer and made a list for himself and was about to propel himself down to the lab in Node 2 when his cell phone rang. Expecting it was a call from Ken, Paul was surprised to hear another familiar voice.

"Paul?"

"Lisa. How did you get through?"

"It seems the general got a scare last night, and he's loosened his grip on me."

"What happened?" Paul asked, somewhat worried.

"Rianne didn't wake up from being with us last night until late this morning. It appears the general's staff thought something had happened to her when they couldn't wake her while she was under their care, so they rushed her to the hospital. The general had his lieutenant summon me to the hospital, and that's where I'm calling you from now."

"Your hospital?"

"Yes. I don't think they wanted to compound their problem and make me even angrier by taking her to a different hospital."

"How's Ri?"

"She's fine," Lisa said while looking around, making sure that no one could hear her. "She feels great. But I'm keeping her in here so they don't lock me back up in the house."

"Sorry this has been so hard on you," Paul said apologetically.

"We're fine, Paul," Lisa responded, her tone bright and chipper. "This is a totally unique and awesome situation, and I'm glad to be a part of it."

"You're not afraid?"

"Maybe a little. But I'm excited for the future and all it might bring. Just imagine, Paul, Rianne's children and Nick's children could grow up in a world without violence."

"Or at least a minimum of it. I'm not so naïve as to think it will all disappear."

"But we can hope."

"Hope is good," Paul agreed.

"Do you know when the interview will be?" Lisa asked.

"Already happened," Paul responded immediately. "I actually thought it might have been Ken calling me about it. He sat in on the whole thing."

"Whom was it with?"

"Naomi Roberts."

"Well at least she's fair," Lisa said approvingly.

"Let's hope so."

"Any idea when it's scheduled to air?"

"Not yet," Paul said, smiling at all the questions. "That's what I thought Ken might be calling about."

"Well, we'll be watching, whenever it is," Lisa affirmed.

"That's what I'm afraid of. You'll be watching. Everyone will be watching. And I'm still not one hundred percent sure I've done the right thing."

"You're a good man, Paul. Deep down inside, you're a good man. Hang on to that."

"I'm trying."

Lisa looked up and noticed one of her residents standing in her doorway. "I need to go, love. I'll call you when I can."

Paul's cell phone indicated the call had ended. He still had his doubts, but he was happy to have Lisa's endorsement. It had been his source of strength for many years now.

As Entity had predicted, the alien confiscation of weapons was clearly rubbing nerves raw, and angry, violent threats dominated much of social media. Paul wondered if all this hostility might overwhelm the aliens' formidable power to keep up with events.

Large gatherings of people congregated in cities around the world, but particularly in the United States where the gun-rights activists were strongest. There were large groups of protesters on all sides of the issue—those who wanted to keep their weapons, those who were happy to see them go, and those who simply feared the presence of the alien invaders. Many of those who wanted to retain possession of their weapons were keeping them close at hand, assuming that if they never let them go, they might be safe. But all too often, even in broad daylight, even in the midst of crowds, their weapons continued to disappear, and no one knew how. And all Paul could do was marvel and pray that the aliens would succeed before any more violence erupted.

Nor was it just personal arms that were getting increased targeting. Military weapons systems, though they didn't disappear, continued falling victim to alien manipulation and simply stopped functioning. In response the stock market plunged as companies whose profits were tied to the so-called military-industrial complex struggled to find answers to the devastating alien intervention.

Paul had assumed that Ken Ishida would call him and tell him when the interview would be broadcast, but that call never happened. Others at mission control had been in contact during the afternoon, but everything they spoke of was space station related. From Paul's perspective those aspects of the mission had taken a back seat to what had been transpiring with Entity, and he knew it was time to correct that and get back to the mission at hand. Now that the interview was behind him, he assumed his job with the aliens was finished and life aboard the space station would go back to normal for him, if anything about being in space could be called normal.

Tomorrow was also the day that Martina would be leaving the space station, and Paul spent a good deal of the afternoon helping her stow her gear and prepping for her departure. It was a good reminder to Paul that nothing was easy in outer space.

Afterwards Paul took a little time to water the fruit and vegetable plants that were growing in the lab as part of an array of experiments. By the time he returned to his quarters, Martina was watching the broadcast of his interview, which he then sat down and watched with her. When it was finished, all she said was "Good job," but he was unsure if she really felt that way. Always the confident soldier and astronaut, he was surprised at how hesitant and unsteady he felt about all that had transpired, and the only thing he really wanted to do at this moment was talk to Lisa. Then he thought about a real trip to Mars, and the notion of being totally out of contact from loved ones was sobering. As a consequence he did his best to put those thoughts out of his mind.

"I hope I didn't say anything to affect our friendship," Paul said as Martina floated by outside his CQ.

"Not at all," said Martina. "I just wish the aliens had chosen me."

"Why is that?" Paul asked, his interest stirred.

"Because you're the first. Like being first to fly. First to cross the ocean. First on the moon. You're the first to communicate with an alien. I think you have been so wrapped up in the issues surrounding this encounter that you really haven't thought about your own place in history."

"As the man who pissed everyone off?" Paul laughed.

"Or as the person who gave humankind a fighting chance," Martina allowed.

"You make it sound courageous, but I feel nothing but confusion and distress."

"That's because you're down-to-earth even in outer space, which shows me that the aliens chose wisely," Martina stated with admiration.

"You think?"

"I'm sure of it." Martina floated into her near-empty CQ for her final night onboard. "Sleep well," she said before zipping it shut. "I'll see you in the morning."

The man had been waiting outside the hospital for several hours. He had been sitting in his car, stewing over the fact that his guns had disappeared, and after watching Naomi Roberts's interview, he held the astronaut personally responsible. How dare this man take away people's right to protect their loved ones.

It had been a difficult time for the man and his family, or what was left of it. He and his wife had lost two children, fraternal twins, in the high school where the shooting took place and Nick was a student. After watching the interview, his only remaining son had stoked his father's resentment by reminding him of the connection between the astronaut and his doctor wife who, as far as the man was concerned, was responsible for letting his daughter die. Given the speed at which the justice system moved in the country, the man was determined to take matters into his own hands and bring justice to those responsible. But he pondered over something the astronaut had said in the interview, that they "try to know what's on everybody's mind."

The man sat in his car, listening to the radio, concentrating on the news and music, hoping it would create enough interference to hide his thoughts. The plan simmering in the back of his mind was to use the car as a lethal weapon, and he assumed that since the car still existed, there must have been some merit in his approach.

He sat there for the entire afternoon and continued on until the sun had set. He sat there ruminating, listening, trying to control his thoughts, but when he finally saw her, all that was cast aside. As she crossed the street to the parking lot where he sat, he turned the ignition key to start the car, fully preparing to run her down. But while the ignition was on, the starting motor failed to engage. This infuriated him even more, and as the woman came ever nearer, the man's anger boiled over, and in a burst of rage, he leaped from the car and ran toward the woman, punching her, choking her, and shoving her hard to the ground, a small pool of blood collecting under her head where it hit the pavement.

He stood over her for a minute, numb, much of his anger subsiding, not sure he had done anything to make himself feel better or bring his dead children back to life. In a state of remorse and confusion, he turned and started walking toward home, only to be stopped by hospital security officers rushing into the parking lot, guns drawn. The man stopped, but when told to lie down on the ground, he refused and just stood there.

A small crowd was gathering in front of the hospital, and emergency-room workers waited for the situation to resolve itself before they felt free to help the victim. Suddenly the man yelled and rushed toward the officers, and in an instant, shots were fired. And McKenzie Phillips's father was dead. The incident was over. With that the emergency team hurried to where Lisa lay.

"Dad?" Rianne said over the cell phone, her voice soft and shaky.

Paul was still in his sleeping bag when Rianne's call came through. While news of the incident had been reported on various media outlets, Paul was still in the dark as to what had occurred.

"Ri?" Paul asked, already aware that something was terribly wrong just from the tone of the girl's voice. "Are you okay?"

"It's Mom, Dad," Rianne whimpered, sobbing while trying to maintain her composure. "Somebody hurt her, and she's in the hospital."

"Hurt her? How? Why?" Paul's voice had lost its cool edge as fear and anger overtook him.

"I don't know, Dad. She was coming home, and a man attacked her in the hospital parking lot. The police killed him. That's all I know. But they won't let me see her."

After the initial shock had subsided, Paul did his best to pull himself back together and focus on his daughter's well-being. "Are you all right, Rianne?"

"I'm worried about Mom, Dad."

"Of course you are, but is anybody with you?"

"Nick and Aunt Becca are here with me, and Grandma is talking to the doctor. Mr. Ishida is supposed to be here in a little while too."

"Is your aunt with you now?"

"Yes."

"Would you let me speak to her?"

Rianne passed the phone over to her aunt Becca, an attractive, single, smart attorney in her thirties. Lisa was older by a couple of years, but the two were more than sisters. They were also best friends.

"Paul?" Becca said, rising to try and find a quiet corner to talk in.

"Becca, what's going on? Is Lisa all right?"

"She suffered a severe head trauma, but the doctors hope she's going to be all right, though it may take some time. Our mom is with the attending physician as we speak."

"What happened? Do they know?" Paul probed, still in disbelief.

"She was attacked by the father of the young girl who died while under Lisa's care."

"McKenzie Phillips?"

"Yes," Becca replied. "He had lost a son in that shooting as well. The man's other son told police that he was angry and held Lisa responsible."

"That's ridiculous," Paul said, infuriated that someone could do such a thing. "Surely he must have known she did everything she could to save his daughter."

"You'd think, but apparently not. He was also mad about something else." Becca hesitated.

"That being?" Paul asked guardedly.

"He saw your interview and apparently felt betrayed."

Paul sank into silence. He suspected there might be repercussions, but he never anticipated anything like this. How could he have been as stupid and thoughtless as to put his family into such jeopardy?

Becca could tell from the silence that Paul had taken her telling him about the man's response to the interview personally. While she would have preferred not saying a thing, she knew he would find out eventually, and it was probably kinder to have that information come from family.

"Paul? Are you still there?" she said, trying to coax him back into conversation.

"Still here," he responded quietly.

"You didn't do anything wrong. You know that, right?" Becca said, trying to raise his spirits.

"I have no idea anymore, Becca. All I know is that I wish I were the one who was heading home today rather than Martina."

"Don't say that, Paul. This is what your mission is all about. How someone responds in space when terrible things happen, and they will happen when people go to Mars. You know they will. Lisa is going to be fine. She's tough. And she's surrounded by loved ones, and above all she knows how much you love her. That makes all the difference."

"But I could have prevented this from happening," he replied in sober tones.

"You know, Paul, I know my sister pretty well, and I am certain she would have kicked your butt if you had done anything different. And I just might possibly have helped her."

"Thanks, Becca," Paul said with a somewhat begrudging smile.

"I think your son wants to tell you something, so I will hand the phone to him. He and Rianne and Ralph will be staying with me while Lisa is recovering, and I will keep you posted as to her progress."

"Can I talk to Lisa?"

"She's in a coma, Paul. Maybe tomorrow. I'll let you know as soon as she is able," Becca said, her voice filled with compassion.

"Thanks," Paul responded, totally dejected. News of the coma was not good.

"Here's Nick," Becca said, handing the phone over to the boy.

"Dad?" Nick said, sadness shaking his voice.

"You feel free to call me whenever you feel like, Nick," Paul said, trying to raise his son's spirits while feeling a bit puny himself. "I wish I were with you and Ri and Mom right now."

"I know, Dad. We wish you were here too. But I'm so proud of you for what you said and what you've done. You're awesome, Dad. Awesome! And you're a good man and a good father, and I'm sorry about what happened to you during the war. It wasn't your fault, and I believe in you, Dad. And I love you. And I don't need a gun. I have my family, and that's what counts."

Paul's heart almost broke, and he could feel the emotion welling up in his chest as he struggled for composure. "Thanks, Nicki. You don't know how much that helps to hear." Paul could feel tears filling his eyes, but this time he made no attempt to stop them. "Give your mom a kiss for me. Will you do that, son?"

"Sure, Dad. I'll give her two! Big squishy ones, as Ri likes to say!" The boy was laughing through waves of tears.

"That's my boy." Paul ended the call and looked over at Martina's empty cubicle and experienced a level of loneliness he had never thought possible. He was in a deep psychological hole and wondered if he would ever be able to pull himself out of it. Then he heard Anton's voice over the intercom. It was time to help get Martina dressed and prepped for her ride back down to Earth.

The doctors ran every test possible to ascertain the extent of Lisa's injuries. Beyond the multiple contusions, she had two cracked ribs and a fractured skull and remained in a coma.

The injuries were severe enough to keep her in the ICU with her condition listed as critical. The doctor was finally able to convince Lisa's family members to go home for the evening, assuring them that there was nothing further they could do at the moment and that he would call the moment the situation changed. The only one to ignore the doctor's advice was Nick, who, as he had done with McKenzie, refused to leave the hospital while his mom was in peril. While he was glad he had patched things up with his mom, he couldn't help thinking he wished he hadn't been so condemning and selfish in the first place. Lisa's doctor, aware of the young man's burden, did everything he could to make Nick comfortable through the long days and nights to follow.

Rianne normally looked forward to staying with her aunt Becca. The two got along famously, with Rianne describing her aunt as a "with it" kind of person with plenty of music and board and video games. Becca loved going out to eat, drove a nice BMW convertible, and was really pretty. And she was smart. The two spent hours playing all kinds of games, but their favorite was Backgammon, with the lawyer winning the majority of games. Becca secretly viewed Rianne as the surrogate daughter she would probably never have. She enjoyed the fast life of an attorney, and the money it brought with it, and suspected she was probably never going to settle down, at least not before her childbearing years were over. She loved being around men, all kinds of men, and could not envision settling down with just one exclusively. But as she aged and observed her sister's blissful marriage to Paul, her attitude slowly started to evolve. Maybe marriage would be in the cards, but not today.

Becca had been fascinated by Paul's interview with Naomi Roberts. As close as she and Lisa were as sisters, she still had no idea of the depth of involvement her sister's family had with regard to the aliens. She took the opportunity to cross-examine Rianne for any additional information Ri could provide about her own two visits to the moon. And what Becca heard was truly astounding and made her wish she could go to the moon as well. And she was more than a little annoyed that the furry dog at her feet had actually met a real alien long before she ever would.

Throughout the evening Becca's main goal was to distract Rianne's attention from what was going on outside the house and inside her head. While the girl was normally full of energy and enthusiasm when she stayed with her aunt, on this particular visit, she spent most of her time brooding about her mother. Not only was the country and entire world in chaos, but many people, including some of Rianne's fellow classmates, were holding her father, and by association Rianne herself, responsible for it all. But ultimately it was Rianne and Nick's mother who had paid the highest price.

Becca always enjoyed having Rianne around whenever the opportunity presented itself, but under the circumstances it was very hard for her to keep Rianne's spirits up. Becca had always considered her sister a mentor, and Becca was now deeply concerned about her sister's recovery and the potential challenges Lisa faced in the future.

Ken Ishida had spent a small amount of quality time at the hospital with Lisa's family. He found it deplorable that someone of such value to society would be attacked so brutally, yet he also felt a small amount of sympathy for the man who had lost his life in the aftermath of his crime. Such horrible things had happened to his family in such a short period of time that it was hard to imagine being in his shoes or knowing how anyone would react in a similar situation. But it did seem ironic that the man's anger over the loss of his children to gun violence, and the disappearance of his own guns, eventually got him killed by a bullet. Violence was a curse, and all Ken could do was ponder the absurdity of it all.

Martina's journey back to Earth went off without a hitch, and by now she was preparing to greet her family. That night Paul slept in the crew quarters by himself. It was an odd feeling being alone with his thoughts, with the only other people on board being the Russians at the other end of the space station, almost a football field's length away. He tried going to sleep, but all he could do was think about Lisa and how he wished he could be by her side. Never a deeply religious person, he wondered if God was punishing him for his lack of faith in the past. His attention was so fixed on his wife's condition that he hadn't given a single thought to Entity or the aliens, so it came as a bit of a surprise to him that when he finally did go to sleep, he found himself back on the moon.

"I didn't ask to see you," Paul blurted out as the alien emerged from the fog. He was actually a little angry to be pulled from sleep after working so hard to get some. "And what's with the fog?" he said with irritation. "Can't you just walk into a room on the moon like a normal person?"

"You're angry." Entity observed, responding telepathically.

"Yes," said Paul. "I'm angry. With you. With myself. With the man who attacked my wife. With the interview. With the whole damn world." Paul was exhausted by his anger, but thankfully his mood slowly gave way to the calming effect he normally experienced in Entity's presence. Tranquility cleansed him, and his thinking clarified in direct proportion, though he was still aware of a profound sense of sadness. "I'm sorry," he finally offered the alien.

"There is no need to apologize," Entity said out loud. "Your feelings are understandable."

"So you know what happened to my wife, Lisa?"

"Yes."

"Can you do anything? Bring her up here? Fix her?" Paul pleaded.

"Unlike tapping into the conscious and subconscious parts of her brain as we normally do, we would have to transport her entire body to help her. We don't think that would be wise at this point in time."

"Why not?" Paul demanded.

"Such a trip would be very stressful for her at a time when her brain is busy trying to heal her wounds. We would not want to interrupt that process. So as long as she is in a coma, it is best for her to remain in the care of her physicians on Earth. But should things change we will certainly reevaluate the situation."

"Well, that's good to know," Paul replied, only slightly reassured. Then he changed the subject. "So you must have wanted to see me about something because I certainly don't remember thinking about coming here today with all that's happened."

"That's true. We did."

"So what's up? Did you see my interview?"

"Yes."

"What did you think?" he asked after waiting several seconds for a more complete response.

"We thought it went well."

Paul studied Entity for a moment, sensing something different. "You know, I'm not as good at reading minds as you are, but I can usually tell if someone is holding back on me. What's going on?"

"We think we made a crucial miscalculation," Entity said slowly, but with absolute conviction.

"What do you mean?" Paul asked, surprised by the alien's candor.

"We think you may have been right. That we should not have tried to intervene in your planet's struggles."

"What changed your minds?" Paul said, trying to figure out where all of this was leading.

"We have helped many civilizations over time and have come to anticipate some level of resistance. But we have never felt such outright hostility toward what we were doing as we have witnessed on Earth."

"I tried to tell you," Paul responded, feeling slightly vindicated.

"You did," the alien acknowledged. "It seems we should have listened. We knew there were serious problems from the broadcasts we intercepted, but we had no way of knowing how extremely volatile your society actually is."

"So what are you going to do about it?" Paul asked, fully expecting some change in tactics.

"We are going to attempt to return things back to the way they were. At least to the extent possible."

"What?" Paul said, feeling like he had just taken a punch to the head. "Why?"

"We've decided we should leave." There followed a long moment of silence.

"Who decided? The only one I ever see is you."

"The group decided. All of us who do this kind of thing. We all felt that maybe we were wrong when it came to helping Earth."

"Why would you do that after coming this far?" Paul asked in disbelief.

"Your wife is a good person and a good doctor, and yet someone tried to kill her, in part because of your association with us. There are whole factions on your planet who are fighting each other because of us. We've become the catalyst for the very behavior we are trying to prevent."

"But you said it yourself. It's a slow and difficult process."

"The slow and difficult process we spoke of was in reference to a projected decrease in violence. But in actuality thoughts of violence on Earth have increased substantially as a result of our actions, and we feel compelled to rethink what we are trying to accomplish here. Your species is considerably more aggressive than any other intelligent life we have ever encountered. "

"You mean all those alien movies were wrong, huh?" Paul said. "All those aliens weren't out to try and kill us."

"No," Entity responded telepathically. "Why would anyone want to kill you after searching so long to find you? It makes no sense."

"But suppose they were much more powerful than us," Paul ventured, sounding almost like a kid. "Maybe they just want to mine our minerals."

"If an ant walked up to you and spoke to you, would you step on it?" Entity posed.

"No." Paul understood where Entity was coming from, and his heart felt sick. For the first time in his life, he was ashamed to call himself human. "Violence and anger *is* increasing because of what you are doing and may even get worse for a while, but you've got to keep things in perspective. It's true that Earth can sometimes be a vicious place. But it's also a beautiful place, populated by many loving people. And I think you were right about giving Earth a chance, but that's a long-term objective, not a short-term one." He drew close to the alien and thought he saw sorrow in Entity's eyes. "Almost everything that's worthwhile is difficult, and what you have been proposing may be the most difficult thing of all: changing the core of who we humans are."

"But we never intended to cause pain. To do so is to go against everything that *we* are."

"I understand. But you most of all should know that there will be pain now whether you stay or go. There may be some people who are angry with you now, but there are many others who I am sure will be angry with you later should you decide to leave. I am sure there are more people who want what you are offering than those who don't, but those who don't are not going to disappear without a fight. It's their nature, but hopefully they won't have their guns.

For the first time since encountering the alien, Paul saw the anguish Earth was causing this placid race, and he felt sorry for their involvement and equally grateful for it.

"A while back you asked me to make a choice, and now it's your turn," Paul said supportively. "I'm asking you not to give up on us. I'm telling you we are worth it. I believe it, and I want to know you still think so too. You may be able to return things back to the way they were, but I don't think it will ever be the same for me or for the rest of my kind. Not really. You've let us see the light. To realize what's possible. You can't take that away from us now."

"The decision has been made," the alien said flatly.

"Then unmake it! Naomi Roberts said I give up easy. Well, what about you? What kind of advanced alien race are you that you would get us halfway to peace and then quit?

Entity did not respond. Not out loud. Not in Paul's head. Entity disappeared, and seconds later Paul was back inside his sleeping bag in his CQ.

When Paul woke the next day, it took several minutes before what had transpired that night came back to him, but when it did it hit him like a ton of bricks, and he had no idea what to expect. Had the aliens really packed up and left? Was it possible for them to leave Earth the way they found it, or would competing human factions become even more polarized in the aftermath of the alien experience? Would gun-rights advocates, so many of whom felt that the earth had been attacked in a *War of the Worlds* different kind of way, fight to make sure that something similar could never happen again?

Paul had great difficulty putting these thoughts out of his mind. He forced himself from his sleeping bag, used the WHC, and then checked his Short Term Plan Viewer for his daily assignments. His thoughts turned to Lisa and what she was going through, and he felt nothing short of impotent. It was at that point that his cell phone rang.

"Dad?"

Rianne's voice surprised Paul, and his heart skipped a beat, half expecting bad news about Lisa. "Ri, how's your mother?"

"Mom's still asleep, Dad. But I did smooch her for you, but just once. Nick told me I should do it twice, but I thought I'd wait until she woke up before I do that."

"You should smooch her as often as you want, Ri. It's possible she is fully aware of what is happening, and she'd probably appreciate your kisses."

"I'll do that, Dad, but I'm not at the hospital anymore. Since Mom was still sleeping, Aunt Becca and I came back to her house to watch what's happening in Washington, DC, and some of the other big cities around the country." Rianne sounded very enthusiastic.

"What's going on, Ri?" Paul asked quizzically.

"I don't know, but the aliens have moved their buildings to Earth."

"What do you mean?"

"There's an alien building on the Mall in Washington, like the one we saw on the moon. And there are others in New York, Chicago, Houston, Los Angeles, Seattle, and other cities."

"Ri, is your aunt there?" Paul asked, dumfounded and excited, both at the same time.

"I'm here, Paul, on speakerphone."

"What's going on?" Paul questioned Becca as he fumbled to bring the laptop in his CQ online.

"Apparently the aliens have established some kind of network in all the major capitals and cities of the world."

"For what? Does anybody know?"

"I don't think so, Paul. But word is that the rate at which weapons are disappearing has increased, and the major military powers are on high alert. But none of them are sure their weapons systems would actually work should they be called upon in war."

By this time Paul had CNN on his screen and was watching the same news feeds that Becca and Rianne probably were. Rianne and Becca were absolutely correct in that the building on the Mall was an exact duplicate (or perhaps not even a duplicate) of the cathedral-like structure he had been in so many times on the moon. "So they decided to stay," Paul whispered under his breath.

"What was that, Paul?" Becca inquired.

"It's not important," Paul said and then quickly changed the subject back to Lisa. "I haven't heard a word from anyone at the hospital yet. I assume they have my number."

"I think they're a little intimidated to call the space station. You're a famous astronaut, you know," Becca quipped.

"But I'm still Lisa's husband."

"I know, Paul. It can't be easy for you," Becca said sympathetically. "Dr. Allen is the doctor treating her. He's their top head-trauma specialist. I spoke with him this morning, and when I go back this afternoon, I'll be sure to tell him to call you."

"Thanks. I'd appreciate that. But what did he tell you this morning?"

"Nothing much new. She's still in a coma, but they did do an fMRI scan." Becca hesitated.

"And?" Paul queried.

Becca stood up and looked over at Rianne, "I'll be right back," she told the girl before she disappeared into the kitchen. "Sorry, Paul," she said, taking the cell off speakerphone. "I had you on speakerphone, and I didn't want Ri to hear this."

Paul braced himself for the worst. "Go on."

"At this point there doesn't seem to be much activity in her brain, Paul," Becca said, trying her best to soften the blow. "The doctor said there is a profound disturbance of consciousness."

"What the hell does that mean?" Paul's voice was filled with worry.

"She's in a coma, Paul. That means there's no eye opening or recognition of surroundings. It's not even at the level they call a vegetative state."

"Does that mean she's going to die?"

"I think it means there's no way to tell right now. She could transition into a vegetative state within days where she becomes more aware and eventually starts to regain some of her cognitive abilities. Or she could stay in a coma for much longer. In that case things could be quite different. She could develop a respiratory illness or some other life-threatening complication. The point being, all we can do is wait and hope and pray."

All Becca heard on the other end of the phone was silence. Finally she said, "Paul, I'm so sorry I had to tell you this."

"It's okay, Becca. I had to find out sometime, and I'd rather hear it from you than just about anybody else." Paul was feeling faint for the first time in his life. All he wanted to do was crawl into a hole and lick his wounds. "I think I'll hang up for now," he said, trying his best to maintain his composure. "Please tell Rianne I had an emergency and had to take care of it. I don't think I could talk to her right at this moment and pretend to be uplifting. Maybe later, but not now."

"I understand, Paul. And I'll talk to Rianne, not to worry. We're doing fine." Then she added, "I'm so sorry."

"I know. But I also know this is happening to you, and I am grateful that Lisa has you since I can't be with her."

"Thanks, Paul," Becca said wiping tears from her face. "I'll call you tomorrow."

Paul ended the call, looked around the empty crew quarters, and wept.

The segments of the alien population who were involved with planetary social modification were spread across the universe, but simultaneous communications with all individuals was possible since their highly developed brains had long ago evolved to use quantum entanglement as a means to communicate and disseminate information. This form of communicating information had the added feature of doing so without time considerations. Spooky action at a distance, as Einstein had called it, was harnessed giving the aliens the ability to do an end run around relativity.

Entity communicated the present circumstances that were consuming Earth's populations to colleagues, as well as the argument that Paul had put forward to Entity concerning the alien's leaving, and after many thoughts going back and forth, there was consensus that the aliens should stay and keep the operation moving forward. But they also recognized a need to change their strategy. Though the idea of using any type of coercion was abhorrent to the aliens, even though it seemed like the only thing that some on Earth understood, the notion of using their vast power and technology in some overwhelming but peaceful way was not out of the question. They could most certainly devise a way to entice humans to change and watch over them for as long as it took to alleviate any outbreaks of violence. Thus the collective minds of the aliens began to formulate a plan.

Ken Ishida stopped at the hospital on his way to Galaxy that morning to visit the woman who had saved his wife's life a few years before. He arrived early, only to find the room empty. Wondering what had happened, he asked the nurse at the duty station. The nurse informed Ken that Lisa had passed away earlier that morning and called for Dr. Allen to come speak to him.

When the doctor arrived, Ken explained who he was and his connection to Lisa. Dr. Allen was aware of the delicacy of the situation and told Ken that he intended to call Paul himself but had delayed doing so because he had concerns about Paul's overall state of mind under the circumstances, adding that he was thankful Ken was there to speak with him. Ken assured the doctor that Paul was an extremely resilient individual, but he admitted that this was going to be an unprecedented blow for the astronaut. He suggested that, as mission commander, maybe he should pass the news along to Paul. The doctor not only approved but seemed somewhat relieved to hand the responsibility over to Ken, though he did reassure Ken that should Paul want to speak with him directly, he would be happy to do so.

Ken asked the doctor whether he had informed Rianne, Nick, Becca, or anyone else in the families, and the doctor assured Ken that doing so would be his next task. As the conversation drew to a close, it was evident to Ken that the entire hospital staff was experiencing a profound sense of loss. Lisa had been a great doctor and a good friend, and it was going to be a tough day for everyone.

Ken arrived at Galaxy a short time later and spread the word about Lisa's death but asked that everyone there keep the news under wraps until Paul had been notified. When they heard the news, John Wilner and Dr. Price asked Ken whether he was going to offer Paul a ride home should he want one. There was a lot riding on the mission, and the cost would certainly be steep, but they had to consider the possibility. While the mission was simulating what might happen while on a trip to Mars, there was no getting around the fact that this was not an actual mission, and to deny Paul that option would be cruel. There was no conceivable way, however, for Paul to get back to Earth in a reasonable amount of time. But it would be possible for the funeral to be postponed until he arrived. No matter the solution, it would be difficult.

Ken called Paul later that morning, and as expected Paul was devastated when he heard the news, yet he talked about sticking with the mission. Ken found himself in a difficult position. He knew the family circumstance, that Rianne and Nick probably needed their father now more than ever. While Becca was a terrific aunt, at this moment she was no substitute for an actual parent if one was available. On the other hand, there was valuable data to be mined should Paul choose to stay onboard the space station. The question became, would Ken's conscience permit him to let Paul do such a thing? Before the call ended, Paul and Ken agreed to sleep on it since nothing they did today would change anything.

After the call had ended, Ken discussed the matter with Dr. Price, whose professional opinion was that it was too soon to tell. Waiting until morning would hopefully provide them with more information about Paul's mental state. It would also give Paul an opportunity to contact Rianne and Nick, at which point the entire picture could change.

Ken had given Paul the go ahead to use videoconferencing to contact his children. But by the time Paul spoke to them,

Rianne and Becca had already been to the hospital and, with Nick at their side, had already spoken with Dr. Allen. Not only were Rianne and Nick with their aunt now, they were also with their maternal grandmother. It was a good thing, for they were both shattered by the news of their mother's death, and it was hard for Paul not to feel a sense of guilt for all that had transpired. On two separate occasions, he could have brought the whole thing to a halt, he told himself, but he didn't, and that decision had cost Lisa her life.

Paul's conversation with the children included a discussion about whether Paul should come home or not, but both were adamant that their father remain aboard the space station. With stoicism they assured him they would be all right and that it was necessary for Paul to see the mission through. "That's what Mom would have wanted you to do," Nick insisted. And although Paul appreciated his son's support, he had difficulty knowing what the right thing to do was. He found his feelings so jumbled that every time he thought he had made up his mind, to go home, or to stay, a half hour later, he would find that he had changed it again. As he moved from one state of mind to another, it was hard for him to tell if he was glad to be alone during this time of sorrow or whether it would be better to have the support of fellow astronauts. He thought about going down to the Russian section, but his Russian was not good enough, nor was their English good enough, to make it all worth the effort. He had been through some pretty rough times in his life, but this was certainly the roughest of all.

Paul tried to still his mind for hours but to no avail. He finally decided to raid the medical kit and took a double dose of sleeping pills, finally falling into a deep sleep a short while later.

The ringtone of his cell phone was the first thing the astronaut heard in the morning when he woke from sleep. He was feeling terribly groggy from the medication he had taken the night before. At first he was not even aware it was ringing, and then it took an extra moment to locate it.

"Hello," he mumbled as he fought to clear the cobwebs.

"Paul, this is Becca. Are you all right?"

"Other than feeling like I've been run over by a truck, I'm okay. How are you and the kids?"

"We're doing as well as could be expected. Mom's cooking for us, so at least that burden is off our shoulders, and she seems to welcome staying busy. It keeps her mind off things."

"That's good. I'm still trying to decide if I should arrange to come home or not. I told Ken I would call him today to let him know my decision. I'm grateful they're willing to at least consider the possibility."

"Paul, there's something I need to tell you that may affect your decision."

"What's that?" Paul asked, unsure if he was sensing concern or excitement in her voice. After learning about Lisa's death the day before, he had a hard time imagining that today's news could possibly be worse than yesterday's, but he braced himself anyway.

"Lisa is gone, Paul."

"What do you mean gone?"

"Dr. Allen got a call from the hospital morgue this morning and was told that Lisa's body had disappeared."

"To where?" Paul asked her, still trying to wrap his head around the news. All kinds of thoughts were whirling around inside his brain, from thinking maybe people angry about his interview stole the body, to the possibility that she was actually still alive and the doctors had just made a terrible mistake. Deep in his mind though, he knew both of these scenarios were deeply flawed.

"No one knows. They did call the police to investigate, but apparently they haven't found a single clue as to how, or when, Lisa's body disappeared."

"Don't they have security cameras?" Paul asked.

"They do, and that was the first thing they checked, but there was nothing."

"That's crazy," Paul responded, appalled that anyone would do such a thing.

"I know, Paul."

"How are Rianne and Nick taking the news?" he asked.

"Nick's at your house. He wanted to be by himself after the news of Lisa's death. I don't imagine he knows about the disappearance yet. Rianne is still asleep. But I was thinking I wouldn't tell her until I had to or until the authorities figure out what happened. She doesn't need to add that to the list of things she's worried about right now. As far as she knows, Lisa's body is still at the morgue."

"You're probably right," Paul said. "Use your best judgment."

"I'm sorry, Paul. I wish I had some good news to tell you."

"It's all right, Becca. Everything's all right."

The call was ended on Paul's end, and Becca could only wonder what Paul was feeling, isolated from family and friends in outer space, isolated from the planet, with only a Russian crew onboard, his wife dead, her body missing. If there was a Hell, this could very well be it, she thought. Who would have guessed that Hell would be so far up instead of so far down.

Paul's thoughts, on the other hand, were moving in a very different direction. He started to think about Entity with the specific desire to make contact. Since most of his previous encounters had always come with sleep, he was unsure if such contact was possible while he was awake, but he was sure Entity would hear him. Whether the alien would respond was an entirely different matter.

The cathedral-like structure that materialized in Washington, DC, was the first one to appear, but within days many more like it materialized in capitals and large cities around the world. The structures were like nothing seen on Earth, until now, and were not only extremely large but quite beautiful. Additionally, there was that ethereal quality about them. They were definitely solid structures but appeared to almost shimmer from within, as though the walls were made of paper-thin, translucent metal or graphite material.

In Houston, teams of scientists from NASA examined the structure adorning that city but were unable to draw any conclusions except that it was made of materials not of this world. However, not only were the scientists interested in the secrets the building held, but crowds of spectators gathered near the structure to catch a glimpse of what might lie within. At first authorities tried to keep the spectators at a distance, fearing the purpose of the structure was one of harm. But as soon as they tried to impose any type of crowd control to keep people away, their weapons, night sticks, mace, and Tasers disappeared or stopped working. The message that anthropologists inferred from all this was that the aliens wanted people to enter the building, and soon long lines began to form, leading to the various entrances around the edifice.

The entrances themselves were not solid door-like structures. They were more like curtains of light through which people passed to enter the building. The light curtains were force fields that functioned as screening devices, scanning people's bodies and brains, allowing only certain people into the structure. The criteria seemed to be that people with no weapons or hostile intent had no trouble gaining access. Those with a weapon but no ill intent, who were willing to give up their weapon, could also enter. However, people carrying any form of weapon who did not want to give them up or who harbored any ill intent, were simply turned away, reporting that a horrible odor and high-pitched, persistent screech made staying near the building impossible. Those who were allowed access experienced no such phenomena.

News reporters who managed to pass through the light screens were also welcomed, though their cameras and various recording devices were temporarily deactivated, much to their chagrin. Essentially they were reduced to tourists and experienced only the same privileges as everyone else, though they were certainly free to write about their experiences upon their exit.

The interior of the structure, which on the moon had a central court with trees and creatures from other planets in the universe, seemed to be reconfigured in these buildings to perform an entirely different function. Multiple light-panel displays with images of planets not of Earth's solar system lined much of the interior wall space. The atmosphere these created was reminiscent of a modern airport terminal, apparently intended to seem familiar to the humans now milling about. There were also thousands of enclosed sleeping pods distributed throughout the structure, but their purpose was not readily apparent, and at first few seemed particularly anxious to get into the devices and discover for themselves what that purpose might be. Eventually, however, people would be clamoring for an opportunity to give them a try.

On the ISS Paul had great trouble focusing on his tasks that day. None of his thoughts to speak with Entity had yielded any results. Early in the afternoon, Ken Ishida called asking Paul if he wanted to come back to Earth, at which point Paul informed Ken about Lisa's body disappearing from the hospital morgue. While Ken was appalled, Paul was insistent he stay onboard for the time being. Assuming he could still contact Entity at some point in the future, Paul felt that staying on the space station made a lot of sense. All his previous contacts with the alien had been made while he was on the station, and he did not want to take the chance of breaking that connection. Especially if Entity might be responsible for Lisa's abduction, a secret hope that Paul harbored, which he kept to himself.

However, as the days without any contact from the alien wore on, Paul's hopes began to fade. He could no longer allow himself to hold out for miracles if he was going to be the father that his children so desperately needed now. And at some point he was going to have to tell them about the disappearance of their mom's body. But he would wait until the time seemed right, all the while hoping the police might come up with an answer before that time came.

Several more days passed without a response from Entity, but there were bright spots, especially one particular conversation with Rianne about her mom and how Rianne loved her. Rianne also spoke of her affection for her aunt Becca and dog Ralph. And though the conversation was tinged with grief, happy memories overflowed, and what it communicated to Paul was that his daughter would be all right. Though Paul found his conversation with Rianne difficult in many ways, Rianne's maturity gave Paul strength, and in the end, it picked up Paul's spirits. He was truly proud of her.

Nick was another matter. Though he seemed to no longer harbor the deep resentment toward Paul that he had held previously, he was still noncommunicative, calling Paul only once, and briefly at that. Paul suspected his anger had nowhere to go. With his mother dead, McKenzie dead, her father dead, and his not wanting to alienate Paul again, all his negative feelings turned inward in a struggle against himself. All Paul could do was make himself available for his son to converse with whenever necessary and ask Becca to keep a close watch on his son's state of mind. Should Becca feel that Nick was in any way suicidal, Paul would certainly reconsider his decision about coming home. For the moment Becca felt Nick would pull through just fine. Ultimately he was his father's son, with his father's stamina and strength of character.

Paul also kept track of the latest news from Earth. The disappearance and constraint on weapons that the aliens had begun was now nearly complete. There were still some holdouts trying their best to prevent confiscation of their weapons, but it seemed to most people a foregone conclusion that the holdouts would succumb in the end. Overall, people seemed to be happily enjoying the novelty of the changes happening around them, and things on Earth seemed to be settling down as a new, more relaxed normalcy spread across much of the planet. Paul could only wish that Lisa were still alive to witness the transformation for herself.

A full week later, the mystery of Lisa's disappearance had not been solved, and Paul was still vacillating about whether he should stay on the space station or request a ride back to Earth.

In another week more Americans would be coming aboard to join him, or he could hitch a ride back to Earth on the spacecraft that brought them. It was a difficult decision, but he was leaning toward staying. As he crawled into his sleeping bag and tethered himself in that night, he was struck at how much his thinking had changed over the past week. His emotions, which had been up and down, had settled a little, and he marveled at humankind's resilience in coping with the unspeakable. But it was a small solace because without a doubt, things still hurt like hell.

Paul was able to fall asleep without the aid of pills for which he knew he would be grateful come morning. He had never liked the way most medications made him feel and avoided taking anything whenever possible. But it wasn't long before a voice called out to him in his sleep, and at first he thought it was a dream. But the voice persisted, and when he opened his eyes, Entity appeared in front of him inside his CQ.

"I know you wanted to see me, but I was unable to respond to your requests any sooner." Entity's voice was soft and reassuring inside Paul's head.

"That's okay," Paul said, still half asleep. "I know you're busy saving the world. Which reminds me, I thought you were going to leave it?"

"Even advanced races can change their minds, especially when spoken to from the heart."

"Are you referring to me?" Paul asked rather cynically. "Because I am out of heart these days, maybe for good."

"I think you underestimate your resolve," Entity replied. "And often things are not what they appear."

"What do you mean?" Paul asked.

"I'll show you."

It took only a second for the transformation to begin. It started slowly, first within Paul's CQ, then spreading to the entire node. A fragmentation of sorts was occurring, as though all the atoms composing the space station's exterior were working in unison, allowing Paul and the entity to pass through without obstruction, like a kind of macro quantum tunneling.

Thereafter Paul and Entity appeared to enter a tunnel of light, and within what seemed like a second, Paul found himself inside the central court of a building not dissimilar from the one on the moon, but much larger, this one filled with many others like Entity as well as an assortment of beings that Paul had never seen or even imagined before. What was curious was that everyone seemed to know him and responded to him politely, either out loud or telepathically, before going on about their business.

Entity led Paul away from the center of the structure where they first arrived, to a wall of transparent material, or perhaps a force field, through which Paul could see that the building was set on an entirely different planet. A sumptuous place of lush, multicolored vegetation, varied topography, and a lot of water. To Paul's mind it looked like paradise.

"It's beautiful. But why have you brought me here?" Paul asked the alien.

"Because Entity wanted you to see us."

Paul heard Rianne's voice and turned to find Rianne and Nick standing directly behind him.

"Hi, Dad," Nick said, a huge smile on his face. Paul went to his children and held them in his arms for several seconds, tears of joy rolling down his face.

"I'm so sorry, you two. I feel like I've let you down twice now, big-time." Paul looked over Nick's shoulder and saw Becca standing a short distance away. "Becca, how did you get here?" Paul asked, astonished, but pleased to see her.

"Do you remember those structures that showed up on Earth that look a lot like this place?" Becca related with excitement.

"Yes," Paul responded.

"They are apparently travel portals to peaceful planets. But the only people who are allowed through them are those without weapons or any thought of violence. Basically, people can have their guns or give them up and see the universe."

I thought you were packing heat?" Paul joked with Becca, who for years as an attorney had carried a concealed handgun for protection.

"Not any more. I decided I'd rather shoot for the stars than shoot at targets. Besides, this is way cheaper," the attorney answered with an acerbic sense of humor.

"It's brilliant," Paul commented, more to himself than anyone in particular.

"What's brilliant?" Becca inquired.

"The aliens were going to throw in the towel last I talked to them. They were so distraught about Lisa's death and everything that was happening on Earth. But I pleaded with them not to give up on us, and I think they listened. They created a bargaining chip."

"What do you mean, Dad?" Nick asked.

"They offered us something that everybody loves to do, Nick. In exchange for violence. Travel."

"Even better," Becca added, "you don't need money, there aren't any baggage fees, and the only requirement is that you be nice. I love it."

"It's truly brilliant," Paul said once more.

"Do you think that people will turn in their guns, Dad?" Rianne asked innocently.

"Maybe in time, Ri. But probably not right away. Old habits die hard."

Paul was aware that Entity was standing there all this time, not saying a thing. "I'm sorry. I didn't mean to ignore you. I should be thanking you, for bringing me here to see my family. At least what's left of them."

"That's actually what I wanted to talk to you about," Entity said, speaking aloud. "I wanted to express my gratitude, for reminding us of what is important—to never stop trying to see the good in others."

"I can't take credit for that," Paul responded.

"You underestimate the power of one individual to change the world," the alien assured him.

"That may be, but it ain't me," Paul joked cynically.

"You just don't see it now," Entity sought to point out. "But if you came back one hundred years from now, you might see things differently. We nearly gave up on you, but you didn't give up on us. With your help, and a very much warranted kick to our behinds, to use a human phrase," Entity added without acrimony, "you now have a system that can hopefully provide the needed incentive to accomplish our original goal, a peaceful Earth, and for that I am most grateful. I am also saddened, because that means my time with you is at an end, and I very much value our relationship."

"Why is it at an end?" Paul asked, already feeling a sense of loss.

"The transport system on Earth is designed to continue the job of monitoring Earth's people as well as to maintain itself in perpetuity. This allows us to move on to other planets in need of help."

"But there's nothing that says you can't come back and visit," Nick pointed out.

"Our timelines are very different, Nick. And where our two timelines cross is nearly at an end, which is a shame since you and I have just met. But before I go I need to give you all something that was taken from you. A token of our appreciation for all you have sacrificed."

Paul's heart skipped a beat as he hoped-against-hope for what might follow. Then he reminded himself to lower his expectations and not expect miracles. In reality, he had no idea what to think, and the polite person his mother had raised him to be was just about to say that a gift wasn't necessary when he heard Lisa's voice emanating from the building's center court where he and Entity had arrived.

"Paul."

Paul turned and saw Lisa standing there, fully radiant, looking as though nothing had ever happened to her. Paul walked toward her slowly and enveloped her, kissing her on the face and lips. A moment later Rianne and Nick joined them and finally Becca, in a group hug for the ages. After several moments, with his arm still around Lisa, Paul turned back to Entity. "I can't thank you enough," he said to the alien, doing his best to hold back a torrent of emotions.

"No thanks is necessary. It was the least we could do. Just follow the instructions we gave you."

"I will," Lisa assured Entity."

"What instructions?" Paul asked suspiciously.

"The ones that will keep me alive, sweetheart," Lisa said matter-of-factly. Then turning back to Entity, she added, "I'll let you know if there is anything else I need."

"How will you do that?" Paul questioned her.

"You're not the only one who can talk to Entity you know," Lisa chided with some irritation, making it clear she was done with all the questions.

Paul just shook his head, not understanding, but not wanting to seem ungrateful, happy in the end to accept whatever it meant.

"Mom, Ralph is back on Earth," Rianne said with a tug on Lisa's sleeve.

"Are you saying it's time to go," Lisa inquired of her daughter, who shook her head enthusiastically.

"What am *I* going to do? Paul asked, as though a new reality was dawning on him. "I don't really need to go back to the space station anymore when you think about it. It's like everyone's an astronaut now."

"We can explore space together, Dad," Rianne proposed gleefully.

"Hey, what about me, punk?" Nick protested as he poked his younger sister in the ribs.

"You can do that," Entity explained. "But traveling by way of the transport systems on Earth, as we set them up, is limited."

"How so?" Paul inquired.

"They use the same means I used to transport you to the moon and to here. On those visits we did not move you, we moved your mind. Coming here may have seemed different to you because I allowed you to be fully conscious when I took you from the space station."

"So you're saying I'm still back on the space station as we speak? Just like before?" Paul asked.

"Yes," Entity replied.

"And is that the same for all of us now, as we stand here on this planet?" Paul probed further.

"Yes. Your family must return to Earth the way they came, through the transport system, because like you, their actual bodies aren't really here. You see, we send only your thoughts through the space-time interface, so relativity has no effect on your physical body. Consequently, Earth must always remain your point of origin. But Lisa's actual body had to be physically brought here for reparations."

"And how does she get back to Earth?" Paul wondered.

"The way she came. Through a slightly different procedure. Unless she decides to stay," Entity responded.

"But I thought you said . . ."

"Paul, don't worry about all the science," Lisa teased. "Of course I want to go back. It's not a difficult decision to make," she added without hesitation. "Earth is where our families are."

"I thought that would be your response," the alien said with warmth. "Come, I will arrange to send each of you back as appropriate." Entity led the family to the center court where they had arrived and then backed away slightly. "Are you ready?" Entity asked one last time.

"No. I'm not," Paul blurted out. "I'm going to miss you. A lot."

"It's a probabilistic world, you know," Entity responded. "There is always a chance we will meet again."

"But not soon enough," Paul agonized. "You've done so much to try and help our planet."

"We only did part of the job," Entity confessed. "The rest we must leave to you."

"We'll do our best," Paul promised. "I know I will."

"I believe you," Entity said with quiet assurance while taking one long last look at her friends. Then the entity smiled and added telepathically, "It has been my great pleasure to know you. I hope we do meet again sometime. My blessing to you all." And with that the family was gone.

That afternoon Lisa found herself back home, wondering how she would explain to the hospital staff that she was still alive. Given all that had transpired over the previous weeks, however, she was relatively sure that no one was going to question anything. As for the rest of the family; Becca was back at work, Rianne was back with Ralph, Nick was playing video games, and the soldiers were long gone from the house. The reporters were gone too, but they would no doubt be back. For the moment, however, things at home were pretty much back to normal.

Paul was back on the space station. From the aliens' point of view, alternative methods of development always yielded different, oftentimes better results, and given the restrictions of the transport system the aliens had fashioned, it was in Earth's best interests to continue on its own path of exploration. It seems Paul was still important to the future of human space explorers.

That afternoon when Ken Ishida videoconferenced with Paul, he knew nothing of Lisa's recovery or the fact that Paul had actually been off on some other planet. But nothing seemed to shock Ken anymore. He had already decided to make a pilgrimage to the alien structure in Houston and experience some of what everyone else was talking about—travel to other worlds. He could already feel positive changes happening on Earth, though all the planet's problems were far from being totally solved. But things were definitely improving, and optimism was spreading.

"It's a shame we couldn't solve the problem of violence for ourselves," Ken noted in a videoconference with Paul.

"It's a sad fact," Paul responded, "but I am hopeful. For the moment."

"I am too, Paul," Ken said. "But it's a little like cancer. Once you've had it, even if the doctors tell you it's gone, it's still always on your mind."

"There's something else that worries me," Paul said, ruminating on the potential pitfalls. "There are going to be a lot of industries that will lose big money because of this and a lot of angry people as a result."

"Let them be angry," Ken said with a laugh. "But you can bet those same people will also be the ones who, down the road, cash in on all the new things they discover on other worlds. Money tends to heal a lot of wounds."

"It's possible. I suppose what's important is that we have peace today, and hopefully we will have it tomorrow. And if we shouldn't, hopefully we will see these aliens return."

"It would be nice to think," Ken reflected.

"I'm struck by the last thing Entity said to us."

"What was that?" Ken inquired.

"Entity said 'My blessing to you all.' It never occurred to me to ask about their faith. Religion seems so antiquated for such an advanced race."

"Or maybe it was their faith that allowed them to advance?" Ken countered.

"Now there's something to ponder," Paul said. "I'll talk to you tomorrow."

"Peace, brother." Ken said. "Semper fi."

"Semper fi, my friend."

Paul shut his computer down and decided to take the rest of the day to himself. Usually he would go to the ISS's cupola where he could ponder the beauty of the earth and humankind's insignificance. But the aliens had changed all that. They didn't view humankind as insignificant. They viewed humankind as unique and, in the end, worthy of their time and efforts.

Today Paul went to a different window and peered out at the moon, thinking only of the friendship he had made, still questioning if it was truly real, and hoping against hope that it all wasn't simply a dream. Perhaps humankind did have a future. And perhaps, just perhaps, Paul had actually helped that future along.

The aliens prayed for humankind's future as well, disappointed they could not do more. They also hoped it would take Paul many years before he would discover his wife's secret, that she was a replica. Perhaps by that time he would realize that thoughts and feelings can live on, even when bodies don't.